VANILLA CHAI AND A VANISHING VICTIM

A WATERWHEEL CAFE MYSTERY

VICTORIA TAIT

KANGA PRESS

Dedication

A huge thank you to Sharmani for her enthusiastic help with this book, and the whole series.

A Kanga Press Publication © 2023

Cover Design by Daniela Colleo of StunningBookCovers.com
Editing Allie Douglas

For more information visit VictoriaTait.com

CHAPTER ONE

Thirty-three year old Sergeant Keya Varma slumped into her office chair in her team's room on the ground floor of Cirencester Police Station, in the English Cotswolds.

She removed her flat-topped black hat, with its black and white chequered banding, and placed it on her desk, on top of a pile of paperwork.

"Here you are. Vanilla chai, as requested," said the motherly figure of Inspector Sue Honeywell, setting down a mug of tea on Keya's pale wood-effect desk.

"Thanks," Keya replied as she untied her bun, allowing her long black hair to fall freely down her back. Feeling clammy, she pulled at the neck of her tight-fitting white shirt, wishing she could loosen her black and white tie.

Outside the sun was shining, and the July temperature must have been in the mid-twenties. Inside the modern blue-carpeted, fake Cotswold-stone clad police station, it felt even hotter.

Inspector Sue looked more comfortable in her floaty floral dress, although her face was still flushed. With just two years left until her retirement at sixty, the grey-haired police officer had recently joined the team from Gloucestershire police headquarters.

Keya wondered if, with Inspector Sue's experience of working with families and victims of crime, she'd been appointed to provide balance in their team. And perhaps to bring a softer side than that conveyed by their boss, Inspector Evans, an often cranky Welshman from the old school of policing.

Inspector Sue sipped her tea and said, "This flavour is quite refreshing for a baking summer afternoon. Are you thinking of serving it in your cafe?"

Keya sat up and tasted her tea. She allowed the sweet, slightly floral flavour to linger in her mouth before she replied, "Yes, but it might be better served cold, as iced tea."

Inspector Sue nodded and then said, "I think that went well today. The majority of the children paid attention."

"Mostly those who come from broken or troubled families," Keya responded, dully. "They know that it's the people closest to them, usually their parents, who pose a far greater risk to their safety than strangers." Keya tied her hair back in a ponytail.

"Still, I think we are getting across the government's new message, 'Clever Never Goes', and the children will be more aware of the potential dangers of abduction and online grooming."

Keya wasn't so sure, but she kept her thoughts to herself. Most children were wary of strangers, even though they were often the ones trying to help.

Nowadays, kids rarely got into cars with people they didn't know. But if an estranged parent turned up and offered to take them to McDonalds, or for an ice cream, would they really say no?

"Only Stratton Primary School left to visit tomorrow before the schools break up for the summer holidays," Inspector Sue said in an upbeat voice.

"Hurray," replied Keya flatly. "Then I can try to get to the bottom of this paperwork before I leave on Friday."

"Of course, your sister's rearranged wedding is next week. Is she excited?"

"Yes and no. Zivah used the excuse of moving the date and venue to pare down the guest list, with her fiancé, Aadi's, support. They spoke to both sets of parents and explained that this was their special day, and that if their parents wanted to invite great aunt Fatima, or cousin three times removed Daksh, then the couple would willingly attend a separate party, which their parents could organise."

"Good for them."

"Which means Zivah is excited but in a happy, less manic way. And everything is organised and ready to go."

Constable Ryan Jenkins, who was sitting behind the desk opposite Keya's, answered his mobile phone. "Ozzie! How's life in the big city?"

"Ozzie Winters, the reporter," mouthed Keya at Inspector Sue.

"Of course," whispered back the older police officer, nodding her head.

Ozzie had covered a recent case Keya and Inspector Sue had both worked on. It had given her the big break she'd been seeking, leaving behind the Cirencester Times to write for a national magazine in London, but continuing her freelance coverage of the most current, newsworthy cases.

"Yes, I have seen the girl on the news. She's from Sussex, isn't she? Why do you think she might be in Gloucestershire?" Ryan said into his phone.

He listened before replying, "And they tracked her mobile phone to a service station on the M4? That makes sense."

"I better check my emails," Inspector Sue said in a hushed voice. "If the Sussex police do think that missing girl is in our area, then they're probably trying to contact me."

Inspector Sue moved across to the desk next to Keya's which, until a few weeks earlier, had been occupied by Sergeant Nick Unwin. Nick had made himself unpopular in the station, not just for his overambitious attitude, but also for wrongfully arresting Dotty Sayers, a friend of Keya's and Ryan's, in the spring.

Keya was pleased he'd found himself a position in the regional media team, and remained on civil terms with him, as she never knew when she might need his help, although she wasn't sure about his promotion to inspector. And she couldn't bring herself to forgive him for Dotty's arrest.

It was the way he'd turned on her loyal, kind friend, treating her disrespectfully and with disdain. That had been unnecessary, and his shifting loyalty had been misplaced. The police officer whose coattails he'd been riding on had been exposed for fraud and persuaded to take early retirement.

Which was one of the reasons Chief Inspector Greg had recently been appointed to run the station. He'd been Inspector Sue's boss in the regional Missing Persons Unit, and she'd moved across to Cirencester with him.

The bald-headed Chief Inspector appeared in the open doorway and stared at Inspector Sue. When she looked up from her computer screen, he said matter-of-factly, "Can I have a word?"

As Inspector Sue left the team room, Ryan finished his call.

"How is Ozzie?" Keya asked.

"Good, I think, although I get the impression her magazine work gets in the way when she's chasing a breaking news story."

The office door next to Ryan and Keya opened, revealing Inspector Evans, who closed his eyes, took a deep breath, and then asked hesitantly, "Everything all right out here?"

Keya glanced uncertainly at Ryan, who replied, "Yes, sir. All under control. How's your mum?"

"She insists she's fine, but the neighbour who found her called her doctor who's been to visit. Nothing's broken. This time."

"That's a relief," said Ryan, cheerfully. His round, youthful face and optimistic outlook were enough to raise the inspector's spirits.

"You're right, Constable," said the inspector, loosening his brown tie. "And it's roasting in here. Anyone fancy an ice cream?"

Keya's eyes widened at this unexpected generosity, but she had to admit, as outdated as many of the inspector's views and methods were, he remained loyal to his team.

"Here you go, Constable." Inspector Evans handed Ryan a twenty-pound note. "I'll have something with chocolate on. And get an ice lolly for Stan. He must be melting in the archives."

Stan Rowbottom, a retired police sergeant, helped them out with research, and other mundane tasks during investigations.

As the inspector's door closed, Ryan rolled his eyes dramatically but asked, good-naturedly, "What would you like?"

Ten minutes later, Ryan returned and offered Inspector Sue a choice of chocolate-covered ice creams. Keya chose the one with additional almond pieces.

In silence, the two women cracked the chocolate coating of their treats and savoured the cool vanilla ice cream.

Ryan closed the inspector's door, having given him his change and ice cream, and asked, "Did Inspector Greg want to see you about the missing girl?"

Inspector Sue replied, "He did brief me on the statement Sussex police have issued, but I don't think that's the real reason he wanted to see me."

"Oh, yes?" replied Keya, but she didn't say any more as her mouth caught a piece of falling chocolate.

She let it melt into a smooth creamy liquid in her mouth as Inspector Sue continued.

"It's no secret the Chief Inspector took this position to save his marriage, after the long hours, and missed school plays and sports matches, during his time running the Missing Persons Unit. But he's still struggling to maintain a work-life balance. The school holidays begin on Friday and his wife wants him to go away to the Lake District with her and the children in a week's time."

"That sounds great," muttered Keya through a mouthful of ice cream. "What's the problem?"

"He feels he can't be away for two weeks when he's just taken charge of the station."

Ryan licked the side of his ice cream before he said, "He does know we managed without a chief inspector for several months, and both you and Inspector Evans are quite capable of handling any cases that come our way. And it's not as if we're inundated with murders and major crimes at the moment. I expect we'll mainly have to deal with tourists losing their wallets and car keys, or bored school children annoying their neighbours or shoplifting for the next couple of months."

Keya licked her wooden lollipop stick clean as Inspector Sue confessed, "I know. I told him all that. And he did accept it, but he's still wavering."

Keya's phone rang.

She checked the screen. It was Zivah.

"Hi, Sis. How's the cafe?"

"Busy. And we're running out of chocolate and strawberry ice cream, napkins, and that lovely yogurt and cucumber sauce you found in the cash and carry. Can you buy some on your way here? You are coming soon, aren't you?"

Keya sat up guiltily. Here she was chatting to her police colleagues and indulging in an ice cream while her sister and mother were toiling away in HER cafe.

"Yes. Of course. I'll be right over."

She finished the call and announced, as she pulled herself to her feet, "I have to go."

"Do they need you at the cafe?" asked Ryan.

Keya nodded. "I have to pick up some supplies."

Inspector Sue deposited her ice cream stick in the dustbin and commented, "That's the joy of running your own business alongside your police work, but I've heard good reports about your Waterwheel Cafe."

Keya smiled gratefully and replied, "I'm not sure how I'd manage without my mum and my sister."

CHAPTER TWO

Keya found a space for her metallic reef-blue VW Polo at the back of the car park in front of Akemans antique centre.

The large three-storey Cotswold stone building, and the single-storey auction house next to it, had once been part of a flour mill built beside the River Coln, less than a mile from the village of Coln Akeman.

The door to the auction house was open, and a stream of people were leaving, carrying lamps, rugs, and small pieces of furniture. Today was an auction day.

The antique centre was also popular this summer, in part, Keya hoped, because of her newly opened Waterwheel Cafe at the rear of the centre. The cafe was named after the mill's waterwheel. Keya had organised for it to be restored and it was now the focal point of the cafe, lit up behind large glass windows in the wall facing the river.

Keya, with the help of Gilly Wimsey, who ran the antique centre, had sourced a mismatched collection of outdoor tables and chairs for the patio area so visitors could relax in the fresh air, near the river.

As she and Gilly hadn't yet built a permanent outdoor structure for shade, her resourceful sister had bought huge, sail-shaped pieces of colourful fabric. Zivah had hung these across the space from tall wooden posts with the help of Norman Climpson, the part-time porter at Akemans antique centre and auction house.

Keya carried her first box of supplies through the bustling antique centre. She'd noticed two coaches in the car park and their occupants were mingling with those visitors who'd travelled by car as they perused the rows of booths and concession stalls in the antique centre.

Keya walked down a makeshift corridor, created by the end row of stalls and the wall of the adjoining auction house. Geoff, who displayed and sold military memorabilia, held up his takeaway cup, which Keya presumed he'd purchased from her cafe.

To encourage the stall holders to use the cafe, she'd offered them a fifteen per cent discount, which had proved extremely popular.

"There you are," Zivah declared as Keya entered the cafe, recently converted from the rear section of the ground floor of the old flour mill. Pieces of machinery still occupied space in one corner close to the waterwheel.

Gilly Wimsey had continued the industrial theme installing metal dome pendant lights to illuminate the space, although today sunlight spilled in through the full-height windows overlooking the waterwheel, and the door to the outside patio area.

"We've completely run out of chocolate and strawberry ice cream, and the milkshakes are really popular today. We've even extended the range with the Oreo biscuits you ordered by mistake last week, and my chocolate brownies."

Zivah's hazel eyes shone, as did her sleek black hair, which she'd tied in a makeshift knot on top of her head. It accentuated the delicate bone structure of her face. She was going to make the most gorgeous bride.

"Chocolate brownie milkshake?" queried Keya.

"Yes, it's wonderful and gooey, but rather sickly, but if the customers enjoy it ...". Zivah smiled and took the box from Keya.

After two more trips to her car - she really should find a more efficient way to ferry supplies to the cafe - Keya entered the kitchen.

"My chicken shawarma is really popular," her mother exclaimed, as she wiped her forehead with the back of her arm. She'd tucked strands of her bobbed black hair, with streaks of grey, behind her ears and she looked hot and bothered, even in her saree, but completely at home in the small kitchen.

Zivah had asked for their mother's help to open the cafe, even though Keya had been against involving her. Keya thought her mother would either take over and try to run the operation, or constantly complain about how sore her feet or her back were.

Secretly, she also thought it would be too much for her elderly mother - she was actually only in her sixties - who was already running round and catering to every need of her husband and family.

But it was probably because she'd been doing this for so many years that she was unflappable in the kitchen and able to deal with a myriad of orders.

And she never complained. Keya smiled at her mum, her Amma, who'd transformed into this efficient, energetic, working woman with a new purpose to her life.

The only person who objected to the new arrangement was Keya's dad, no doubt because his orderly life had been disrupted and he had to organise his own lunch.

"That's great, Amma. Which is more popular - the salad or the wraps?"

"Both, I think. And did you bring some more of that mint and cucumber sauce to go with it?"

"I did, and lots of ice cream, although by the list of orders for milkshakes, I'll probably have to order some more for tomorrow."

"We'll also need lettuce, tomatoes, and flour for me to make more tortillas."

"Why don't we buy in the tortillas, so you don't have to make them?"

"Because my fresh ones are so much better, but you do need to decide what to do next week, in the lead up to Zivah's wedding."

Keya glanced through the hatch into the cafe. She had thought that during the afternoon the number of customers would slowly dwindle, but the opposite was currently the case. A small queue was even forming at the entrance as patient customers waited for Zivah to seat them.

What was she going to do next week? Neither Zivah nor Amma

were working, and she wanted some time off herself to prepare for and attend her sister's wedding.

Zivah glanced across and, spotting Keya, widened her eyes, appealing for help.

"I better go," Keya muttered wearily, and left the small kitchen.

"I'll be off then," said Amma.

It was just after half-past five and the cafe was closed to new customers, although some tables outside were still occupied by people enjoying the evening sunshine.

She was carrying a large pink fabric bag over one shoulder and pulling a brightly coloured floral shopping trolley, which she'd persuaded Keya to buy to help her carry ingredients, baking from home, and other items for the cafe.

It was a good idea, and Keya needed to find something similar, if less flowery, for herself.

"Don't spend all night cooking," Keya cautioned.

As Amma left, Zivah, who was leaning against the serving counter, remarked, "You know she loves it. She was born to feed people."

"I just don't know where she gets the energy from. I'm exhausted."

"That's because you've got your police work as well as the cafe, and some of the cases you get involved with are so distressing. It must be mentally draining."

Keya considered this. Not all cases upset her. In fact, she loved her part-time role as Gloucestershire's Rural Engagement Officer, especially liaising with community groups, attending village events, and speaking with the often-uncommunicative farmers in the area.

But she was frustrated by the increasing level of rural crime, which she couldn't manage by herself, and tragedies she witnessed as part of Inspector Evans' team.

"It is, but it's not just that. I thought I'd spend my time at the cafe serving and chatting with customers, or cooking. But I'm mostly preparing orders or physically restocking. And that's before I start on all the admin. And what am I going to do next week when you and Amma are off?"

Zivah gave her a sympathetic smile, but before she could say anything they heard a knocking on the closed door leading into the antique centre.

"Can't they see the closed sign?" Zivah complained.

"It's me," they heard the muffled voice of Gilly Wimsey. "And I've brought Thomas."

"Of course," cried Keya, jumping up. "Gilly asked if I'd give Thomas a job this summer."

Keya opened the door and ushered in the rather shambolic looking figure of Gilly Wimsey with her fifteen-year-old son, Thomas.

Gilly's red tunic style top clashed with her flushed face and ringlets of bright orange hair. "Sorry we're late. Today's auction overran, and a customer complained about …"

"Don't worry," Keya cut in, placing a soothing hand on her friend's arm. "To be honest, we've been flat out this afternoon. Come and try a new flavour of tea I'm considering."

As they walked towards the serving counter, Keya said, "Hi, Thomas," to the stocky, sandy-haired boy.

"Hi," he muttered back, staring down at his feet.

Gilly rolled her eyes. "Thomas, dear, you must look at people when you're speaking to them."

Keya boiled the kettle and made Gilly, Zivah, and herself a cup of vanilla chai flavoured tea. Zivah gave Thomas the banana milkshake a customer had ordered, and then cancelled when she realised she was late collecting her children from a school trip.

Sitting down at a wooden table, Keya asked, "So, Thomas? Why do you want to work in the cafe?"

"Because Mum told me I needed to earn some money," Thomas replied, still not meeting Keya's eyes.

"Well, it is useful to have your own money. But why the cafe?"

Thomas didn't reply.

Gilly sipped her tea. "Interesting," was her only comment as she considered it. Then she said, "Thomas has worked some evenings in the pub washing up, but it's very hot and smelly in the kitchen. And I asked Lorraine in the village shop, but she was rather dismissive. We could try to get him work on a farm …"

Thomas looked up, interested for the first time.

"But he needs to know how to drive a tractor, and neither Peter nor I have time to teach him to drive my little car." Gilly's husband, Dr Peter, ran a surgery out of part of their house in Coln Akeman, and he attended to the medical needs of the residents of the surrounding area.

Thomas' shoulders slumped.

Keya looked at Gilly and said, "We are really busy at the moment. The two students from the village are now adept at using the coffee machine, and they can also make other drinks, help in the kitchen, and wait at the tables. But my biggest issue is that both Amma and Zivah will be off next week, so I'm not sure I can cover for them, and train up Thomas."

Thomas didn't look particularly disappointed, but his shoulders slumped in resignation.

"Why can't I help out next week?" suggested Gilly.

"We don't have another auction until September, and I'm sure Wendy can manage on her own in the auction house, as most items from today's sale will be collected by tomorrow evening. By the way, I bought an oak bookcase which I thought we could use to display some pottery from that lady who visited last week."

"Great idea, and I'd love your help next week, but what about the kitchen?"

"I'm not sure. Let me think about it." Gilly looked directly at Keya and asked, "And Thomas?"

Keya pressed her lips together as she considered the self-conscious teenager. "Why not come in on Saturday morning for a trial? We're not so busy early on, and you can see what you'd like to do. Although you will need to be flexible."

"Will I have to … speak to people?"

Keya smiled understandingly. "Not to start with."

"That's brilliant," enthused Gilly.

"But it's such a shame that Gloucestershire Council won't let thirteen-year-olds be employed. Olivia's dying to work here. Instead, I have to find things for her to do. Dad took her and a friend to Cheltenham's lido today, while I was at the auction, and he said it was rather an eye opener. I'd much prefer Olivia to be here, safely working, than insisting on wearing make-up and mixing with I don't know who at the lido or in Cirencester."

"It can't be straightforward raising a teenage daughter," Keya commiserated.

"Believe me, it's not. Boys are so much easier."

Keya watched Gilly and Thomas leave, thinking back to her school visit during the morning. Were boys less of a worry to their parents than girls? There were so many dangers facing all children.

CHAPTER THREE

It was after nine o'clock by the time Keya reached Cirencester Police Station the next morning.

She'd already spent an hour at home on her laptop ordering resupplies, while munching her toast and enjoying a cup of filter coffee to wake herself up.

Then she'd visited the cash and carry on the edge of Cirencester again, when it opened at half past seven, and delivered more ice cream, fresh lettuce, and flour to the cafe.

She collapsed onto the chair behind her desk in the team room, leaned back, and stared at the ceiling as she yawned.

"Cup of tea?" asked Inspector Sue kindly, from behind the adjacent desk.

"Please." Keya blinked, sat up, and turned to Inspector Sue. "I didn't think it would be so hard. Working part-time and running my café."

Inspector Sue stood up and replied, "But you've been working almost full-time the past two weeks, despite saying you were going to spend more time in the cafe. And the cafe is new and popular, and you're still finding your feet with it."

Inspector Sue left the room, and Keya pondered her words.

She had been going to take time off, but then the team had been instructed to roll out the new abduction awareness message to schoolchildren before the end of term. And having worked on two major cases recently, she was still catching up with her rural engagement work.

Inspector Sue returned with a tray of mugs. She handed one to Ryan, a second to Keya, and the third she picked up and went to knock on Inspector Evans' door.

"Yes," called out the inspector's deep baritone voice.

Inspector Sue opened the door and entered.

"Has Sergeant Varma finally arrived?" Inspector Evans asked gruffly.

Keya groaned. This was going to be a difficult day. She breathed deeply and said, "Yes, sir, I'm here."

"Then please join us."

Ryan returned to his computer while Keya picked up her mug of tea and joined the two inspectors.

"Sue has brought a delicate issue to me, which I thought you might be able to help with, since it involves that meddlesome friend of yours, Dotty Sayers."

Keya's eyes widened. What had Dotty done?

"Only indirectly," Inspector Sue qualified. "But she is in France with Didier Vogt, isn't she?"

Defensively, Keya replied, "She's staying with his parents and helping to look after his twin daughters."

"And do you know how they are?"

Keya narrowed her eyes and looked from Inspector Sue to Inspector Evans, who started examining his fingernails.

Warily she replied, "They are well, and healthy, if that's what you mean? I believe the adjustment from the UK to France has been difficult, which is not surprising after all they've been through. They started at a French school, but I think they're on their summer holidays now. Dotty says the farm where they're living, with Didier's parents, is idyllic and the girls have lots of space to run around."

Inspector Sue nodded but didn't say anything else.

Inspector Evans finished his examination and looked up. Slowly and deliberately, he said, "We were both involved with that case. And the girls' mother's arrest. And as you know, Molly Vogt is serving a life sentence in Gloucester prison." He paused.

"Yes, sir," Keya agreed. "Has something happened?"

"The thing is," began Inspector Sue in a more businesslike manner, "Molly Vogt wants to see her children."

"How?" asked Keya.

"What do you mean?" queried Inspector Sue.

"If the girls are in France, and Molly is in prison, how does she want to see them? By Skype?"

Inspector Sue pursed her lips and wrinkled her nose as she considered Keya's comment. "I hadn't thought of that. But as the girls' mother, she's insisting on visiting rights, but clearly that's not easy. And there are complications."

"What complications?" Keya demanded, becoming frustrated with the conversation. "Surely Molly Vogt gave up her rights where her girls are concerned after committing such a terrible crime."

"Actually, she didn't. She can't. A birth mother has parental rights in respect of her children unless they are legally adopted. She's admitted she knew the girls were going to France but she's cagey about the purpose. As in whether she thought it was just for a holiday, or on a more permanent basis."

"So?" prompted Keya.

"So, technically, the girls are in France illegally, and Molly is accusing her husband of child abduction."

"What? Surely she can't do that?"

"It's not a straightforward law. If she knew and agreed to them going, then she can't claim, under the Child Abduction Act 1984, that Didier abducted them. One parent taking a child abroad without the others consent is wrongful removal and the only legal offence under the act. But as the girls have remained in France, we have to look at this as a wrongful retention case."

"So there's nothing Molly can do?"

"Actually, there is. She can seek a court order for their return, and if her husband ignores it, he will be in breach."

"Which is why," Inspector Evans cut in, "we want to try to resolve this without involving the courts. And your suggestion of electronic contact, in the short term, might just work."

"But what I need to have," continued Inspector Sue, "is an understanding of the girls' current living arrangements, schooling and, if possible, their physical and mental wellbeing."

"Which brings us back to your friend, Dotty," said Inspector Evans.

"Our friend, Dotty," corrected Keya. "Do you want me to contact her?"

"Yes," the two inspectors replied in unison.

Lifting her chin and looking from one inspector to the other, she said, "I'm not going to lie to Dotty, or try to deceive her. It wouldn't be fair, and she would be straight with me in a similar situation. So if you do want me to contact her, I'll have to tell her why."

"You do speak to her, don't you?" Inspector Sue enquired.

"Occasionally, although usually it's a quick text message, as I've been so busy with work and the cafe."

"She's right," nodded Inspector Evans. "Dotty's always been straight with us. We owe it to her to tell her why Sergeant Varma is contacting her."

"But …" began Inspector Sue.

"I know. It will tip Didier Vogt off, and you are trying to handle this discreetly, but I always find honesty the best approach."

Inspector Evans turned to Keya and said, "Please contact Dotty. Tell her you are calling in an official capacity but warn her that if she can't or won't help, lawyers and judges will undoubtedly be involved, which is not good for the girls."

Keya returned to her desk, but Inspector Sue remained in Inspector Evans' office. She closed the door behind Keya, but not before Keya heard her ask, "I know you're loyal to your team, but Dotty Sayers was never part of it …"

"Problem?" asked Ryan, looking up.

Keya wondered how much he'd overheard. All of it by the concerned look on his face.

Ryan said, "If it helps, I agree with Inspector Evans. This is a sensitive issue. Molly is being punished for what she did, but that shouldn't prevent her from seeing her girls. She never did anything to harm them. But Didier has responsibility for them, and he's doing what he thinks is best for them. And I suspect, getting help from his parents. I'm not sure I'd be able to look after two girls full-time."

Keya nodded and picked up her desk phone. She wasn't sure if calling France was included in her own mobile phone contract.

"Hello," answered Dotty's wary voice. She probably didn't recognise the number.

"Hiya. It's me," said Keya, trying to sound bright, but it obviously didn't work.

"Keya. What's wrong?" asked Dotty.

So much for intending to start the call with a general catch up. Instead, she jumped straight in.

"I've just been summoned into Inspector Evans' office." Keya proceeded to tell her friend about the discussion she'd had with the two inspectors.

Dotty didn't interrupt or speak until Keya, slightly out of breath, finished with, "So that's why I've been asked to call you."

"I'd love to catch up properly," Dotty began, "but I can tell you need to sort this out urgently. And you're right. The girls have taken their time settling into life in France. Even though they spoke some of the language, they either didn't, or couldn't, communicate with the other children to start with.

"But Didier's mum is wonderful, and very patient, and between us we've spent time with the girls, shown them around the area, and helped them settle in. The last week of school was a huge improvement and they're loving helping their dad and grandad on the farm at the moment. And you should see them. They're so tanned from spending most of their time outside."

"I am pleased to hear that. I've no idea how they've dealt with the last year and their mum going to prison. But is the intention for them to stay in France?"

"Yes," Dotty confirmed.

"And any plans to visit England?"

"Not at the moment, and I wouldn't recommend it. I think it'll confuse and unsettle them, but I'm not a psychologist. Surely the welfare of the children comes first?"

"I'm not sure. As Inspector Sue said, this is not a straightforward case, but perhaps that's the answer. A psychologist to assess them and give their opinion on the way forward."

The door to Inspector Evans' office opened.

"I better go. Thanks, and you're right. At some point, we do need to catch up."

"I'll be across in Edinburgh soon," Dotty said as Keya put the phone down.

"Well?" Inspector Sue asked, not unkindly, as she moved in front of Keya's desk.

Keya repeated her conversation with Dotty.

Inspector Evans stood in his doorway. "I think a psychologist is an excellent suggestion, Sue."

Inspector Sue nodded. "You're right. You all are. It's the welfare of the children which should come first."

CHAPTER FOUR

On Saturday morning, Keya felt excited. She had the whole day in the cafe.

After speaking to Dotty, she'd spent the rest of Friday at the police station, working diligently through her paperwork and making phone calls.

She still had some left to do, but she could catch up with those on Monday, when the cafe was closed.

After showering and dressing, she decided to skip breakfast and drove straight to Akemans antique centre and auction house.

What a wonderful morning. Rays of sunshine were breaking through the leaves of the ancient, gnarled oak trees lining the narrow lanes. She slowed to pass a woman riding a brown horse and a girl, probably her daughter, on a black and white pony.

Having been brought up in Gloucester, first in a flat in the city centre, and then a house in an estate on the edge of it, she'd grown to love the rolling hills, the abundant hedgerows, and the sheer space of the Cotswolds. No wonder tourists flocked here from all over the world.

She'd started learning the names of the wildflowers and amongst the yellows, whites and blues of those covering the verges, she spotted an orange tortoiseshell butterfly sitting on the purple globe head of a wild clover flower.

Cheerfully, she sang along to the lyrics of *Walking on Sunshine* sung by Katrina and the Waves on a local music station.

Keya had expected to be the first to arrive at Akemans, but she spotted Gilly's little white car in the row of spaces at the front marked 'staff'. Good, that meant Gilly would already have opened up the antique centre.

Inside the cafe, Keya threw open the outside doors to air the space and began by cleaning the tables. Cut flowers were drooping in their assortment of small vases and containers, so, when she'd finished cleaning, straightening and rearranging the tables and chairs, she walked outside to the patio area and descended a set of steps to the riverbank.

Away from the old mill, near the stone bridge which crossed the River Coln, there was an abundance of wild flowers and an area of purple lavender which someone must have planted in the past.

Keya cut stalks of the fragrant lavender, together with delicate blue cornflowers and bright yellow buttercups, even though she knew the latter wouldn't last long in a vase, and returned to the cafe.

"Hi, Sis. Early start?" Zivah greeted her.

"Yes, it's such a lovely day and I get to spend all of it at the cafe."

"Oh good. You can cover for me. I'm going to Cheltenham for a final dress fitting this afternoon in case I've put on weight and my outfit needs some last-minute adjustments."

"Put on weight! You've spent so much time on your feet serving customers, you're wasting away."

Zivah laughed, good-naturedly. "I'm not so sure. I'm rather partial to a slice of cake with my afternoon tea. I brought Amma, and she's already making tortillas. Have you thought about what you'll serve next week? I suggest you keep it simple."

"Good idea. I'll go through the menu this morning. But first, I'll replace the dying flowers with these I've cut, and then I want to put out the display of pottery on that oak bookcase Gilly bought. I see Norman brought it through."

There was a tall, solid wooden bookcase standing against the wall next to the outside door and, beside it, two cardboard boxes of what Keya presumed was handmade pottery from a lady who lived locally.

Keya had intended to open a delicatessen alongside the café, in a purpose built single-storey building. But she hadn't had enough time to source stock, so Ryan had suggested she start with the cafe, and trial some items there, before opening the deli.

Next to the bookcase, a metal shelving unit already contained a display of locally made jams, chutneys, and salad dressings.

An artist friend, Finn, had also asked if he could display some of his paintings, and the abstract images of trees worked well on the exposed brick walls. They'd even sold one of them on Wednesday.

"Here you are. A cup of tea," Zivah said, interrupting Keya's thoughts.

"Thanks, and I better stop standing around and get on with some work," Keya replied, taking the mug from Zivah and admiring the slightly faded floral pattern. All her china was high quality but mismatched. She'd bought some of it from Gilly's Aunt Beanie, and other pieces at very reasonable prices at auctions and car boot sales, or from the antique centre.

Keya arranged the pottery, dusted the jars and bottles on the metal stand, and helped Zivah serve the stream of customers who started arriving as soon as they opened at nine o'clock.

As Keya returned from settling five polite, grey-haired American customers at a table on the patio, Zivah whispered, "I forgot to tell you. Gilly told me she's expecting several busloads of visitors this morning. They're on a tour of the south of England."

"That's good for us, and the antique centre. Fingers crossed we don't run out of stock."

The cafe was already half full when Gilly's Aunt Beanie arrived, escorting a freshly scrubbed-looking Thomas. His hair was shorter than on Thursday evening, and he was wearing a tidy, if slightly too snug-fitting, navy polo shirt and tailored blue shorts.

But Aunt Beanie caused several customers to turn and stare. As usual, she was wearing a headscarf tied with a large bow at a jaunty angle on the side of her head, and today it was a bright, rainbow coloured one.

She'd paired it with a crimson tunic, with purple embroidered flowers, over a pair of purple leggings. Her outfit, together with her somewhat eccentric personality, certainly jazzed up the cafe.

"Here we are," announced Aunt Beanie, "reporting for work."

Keya narrowed her eyes and queried, "Both of you?"

"Yes. Gilly told me you'll be short staffed next week, so I'm volunteering to help in the kitchen. Just tell me what to do."

Keya glanced at the kitchen's open hatch as Amma placed a breakfast sandwich on it. Although Keya's family were Hindus, and vegetarians, they understood the importance of tolerance and that other people had different beliefs and principles. And even Keya's tastebuds were tingling with the smell of frying bacon.

But what would her mother think of Aunt Beanie?

"Um, Mum runs the kitchen. And she's very organised and precise about how she manages things." Which had initially come as a surprise to Keya, but then she was learning many things about Amma, and her relationship with her.

"Excellent." Aunt Beanie stood dramatically to attention, while Thomas cowered behind her, his face flushed. A couple who Zivah was escorting to a table stared. The kitchen might be the best place for an over-enthusiastic Aunt Beanie.

Keya opened the kitchen door and called to Amma. "Aunt Beanie's come to help. Can you show her what to do so as she might stand in for you next week?"

"Of course," her mum called back.

Keya stood back, allowing a bright-eyed Aunt Beanie to enter the kitchen. Then Keya turned to Thomas and said, "Shall I show you how to serve cakes, and make sandwiches from the fillings in the chilled counter?"

Zivah escorted a couple in their early forties to a table close to the long glass-fronted chilled counter. They were accompanied by a younger woman and a toddler.

"Is this table OK, Mr and Mrs Bartlett?"

"And can we have a highchair?" asked the woman, who had large oval eyes, an olive complexion, and wavy shoulder-length dark hair. She was quite small, with an hourglass figure.

It was a good job Zivah had suggested Keya buy a couple of wooden highchairs the previous week. Zivah carried one over and set it beside the woman who picked the toddler up and slid him into it, tightening the nylon straps to stop him from climbing out.

Keya turned to Thomas and explained, "In the morning, we prepare and set out the day's sandwich fillings. These vary depending on the stock we have in and if my mum decides to trial a new filling combination, like this one she's called a northern cheese sandwich filling. It contains grated cheddar, carrot, and onions."

Thomas' brow wrinkled.

Keya rushed on, "But don't worry. We'll keep it simple next week and make sure everything is clearly labelled."

At the nearby table, the woman said, "I'd like a cappuccino and a small portion of American-style pancakes with fruit for my son."

"Don't you think he should just have fruit, Malika?" criticised the man, who Keya presumed was the woman's husband and the boy's father.

He looked scruffy compared with his neat wife, although his t-shirt and jeans were probably expensive, designer ones. He had pale skin and an untidy moustache and beard. But at least his brown hair was tidied up in a bun.

The woman's phone rang, and the man rolled his eyes. "Can't we even go out for morning coffee without being disturbed by your work calls?"

The woman sighed, pressed a button, and placed the phone face down on the table.

"Jonathan, you know my company expects me to be available twenty-four seven for my clients. It's why they pay me so much, and we can only just afford the mortgage on the new house, and Biljana's wages."

The woman looked at the younger woman who was distracting the toddler with a plastic toy, which rattled and jingled.

The man leaned forward and said, "That reminds me. I really think we should upgrade my car. I've found an excellent two-year-old Porsche Cayenne. It's only £75,000."

"Your car? Don't you mean the family car? And what's wrong with our Skoda Octavia? There's plenty of room for all of us and it runs very smoothly."

"It's just, you know."

"No, Jonathan, I don't. And where do you think I can just get my hands on £75,000?"

"Well, there's £48,000 in the savings fund."

"For Zaad's education."

The woman's phone rang again and this time she answered it. As she stood up, she said, "Morning, Amit," and she walked away, towards the open door to the patio.

Keya turned back to Thomas. "Sorry," she apologised. "So, for the sandwiches we have a choice of white or brown bread, or these lovely fresh granary rolls which are delivered each morning. And some customers prefer their sandwiches toasted."

Thomas clutched his right arm, and his eyes were wary.

"Don't worry," she reassured him. "I'll help you with the first ones."

Three young glamorous women, who Dotty would call 'yummy mummies', entered the cafe pushing expensive looking black, baby buggies.

Zivah approached them with a friendly smile and asked, "Where would you like to sit, inside or outside?"

"I think outside," declared one of the women. "But the babies need shade."

"Follow me." As Zivah led the three women through the cafe, Jonathan stood up and greeted the women.

"Hi, Tanya, Emily, Bea."

"Jonathan. What are you doing here?"

"Like you, enjoying a morning out."

"Well we're sitting outside, in the fresh air. It's better for the babies." The woman removed her black and gold sunglasses from her sleek long blonde hair and put them on as she followed Zivah and her friends.

Malika returned to the table and asked, "Who were they?"

"Friends from Bibury baby and toddler group," Jonathan replied.

"And are they the reason you want an expensive new car?" Malika's eyes narrowed.

When Jonathan did not reply, she said, "Perhaps you should try to sell some paintings. After all, isn't that why we had to buy the new house? Because it had a studio for you. And have you sold a single painting?"

"You can't force creativity," rebuffed the man. "I need time to develop my talent. And the right mood and ambience for my art. And I can't display them just anywhere."

"You won't sell any if you refuse to let people see them. So why not start small, and ask the owner if you can display a few here?"

The man sat back, pouting. "I hardly think this is a suitable place for my masterpieces."

CHAPTER FIVE

Thomas jumped and Keya started. Both of them glanced towards the kitchen hatch, through which they'd heard a loud clanging sound.

"Sorry," Aunt Beanie's voice called out.

Keya grimaced. Was it a mistake leaving Aunt Beanie in the kitchen? But she knew the older woman could cook, as she and Dotty had often entertained Keya, Ryan, and other friends at her farmhouse, where both Ryan and Norman Climpson lodged.

Zivah approached and held out an order sheet. She said, "One toasted ham and cheese on white, and a chicken, spinach and bacon roll."

Keya turned away from the kitchen and said, "Here we are, Thomas. Our first order."

She showed him how to make the sandwiches and operate the toasted sandwich grill. While they waited for the ham and cheese toasty, Keya scooped coleslaw into two small white ramekins.

She put lettuce, cucumber, cherry tomatoes, and chopped yellow peppers on each plate to create small side salads, and added a portion of plain crisps.

When the toasty was ready, she cut it into two, creating triangles, and arranged one on top of the other, next to the salad.

"That's how we prepare them," she told Thomas as she glanced up at Zivah, who was serving another table. One of the students picked up a tray from the hot drinks counter where the other student was busy working the large coffee machine.

"And as everyone else is busy, we can take them across to the customers. See, Zivah has written the table number in the top right corner." Keya showed Thomas the order sheet.

As Keya walked around the counter, she glanced towards the entrance. A man with a shaved head, maroon football shirt and tattoos showing on his arms stepped into the cafe and stared around. Keya was about to approach him when, at the table next to her, Jonathan nudged the younger woman, Biljana, and said, "Jason's here."

Biljana stood up, smiling. She waved at the man in the entrance and turned back to the toddler.

"Bye, Zaad. You behave for mummy and daddy, and I'll see you tomorrow night."

"Bye. Have a fun weekend," said Malika as Biljana left.

Keya picked up the two plates of sandwiches and carried them to a table near the glass windows, looking out over the waterwheel.

When she returned, Thomas was holding an order for two toasted sandwiches. One ham, cheese, and tomato, and the other, chicken, cheese, and onion. "Why don't you make these ones?" Keya suggested.

Thomas did well, only needing help with the amounts of tomato, cheese, and onion to add, but the side salad confused him, and he forgot the cucumber and diced pepper.

"Well done," Keya praised him, when he placed the two prepared plates on the counter.

"Now, why don't you take them to the customers? I know you don't want to speak, but just be polite and ask who ordered the chicken and cheese sandwich. Place their plate down, and the other in front of the other customer. There are only the two at that table."

Thomas gulped. "OK," he said hesitantly and picked up the two plates.

"And relax, and remember to smile," added Keya as he crossed the cafe.

The next order was for a slice of lemon drizzle cake and a chocolate brownie. Keya explained the cakes on display to Thomas, and showed him how to serve them.

As he carried the order to a table outside on the patio, Keya glanced around the nearly full cafe and smiled.

At the adjacent table, she heard Jonathan say, "I still think we should upgrade the Skoda. If not a Porsche Cayenne, how about a Range Rover Sport, or a Volvo XC90?"

"Jonathan, the only places you drive are to one of the many toddler groups you insist Zaad needs to be part of, or to one of your 'lunches'. And you don't need a 4x4 for those. The Skoda is more than enough for us."

"But ..."

"Look, we should be saving, not splashing out on expensive items to impress the fashionable mums you mix with. I'd love to offload a few of my clients so I can spend more time at home with Zaad, and perhaps I can take him to one of the groups."

Jonathan's eyes widened. "I'm not sure that's really necessary."

Malika sighed.

"Here's your sister," Jonathan announced, sounding relieved, as the couple were joined by a slightly older version of Malika.

"Thank you so much for having me to stay. I promise, I won't be any bother, but I can't live in the house a minute longer with Xavier, and his overbearing mother."

Thomas returned, and Keya thought he looked pleased with himself.

"Do you think you can manage on your own for a while?" Keya asked.

Thomas' jaw tightened, and he nodded.

"Good. I must see how Aunt Beanie and my mum are getting on."

When Keya opened the kitchen door, her mother was laughing.

"And then she said ..." Aunt Beanie stopped and turned towards the door.

"Wow, it's busy. I have no idea how your mother manages on her own in here." Aunt Beanie turned her attention back to the bacon she was frying, and then she cracked an egg into another frying pan.

"Is everything OK?" she asked Amma.

"Of course. Why wouldn't it be?"

"No reason," said Keya, backing out of the kitchen.

"Keya," called Zivah.

It was time to get back to work.

CHAPTER SIX

The following Wednesday, Keya stopped and checked her reflection in the oval gilt-framed mirror in the entrance bar of The Ivy Montpellier Brasserie, Cheltenham.

Beneath it, there was a huge arrangement of light blue hydrangeas.

She checked her watch. Only fifteen minutes late.

Striding into the main dining room, Keya halted again.

The last time she'd been here was with Dotty, when her friend had undergone her transformation from a self-conscious, timid soul, who hid under shapeless clothes, to a confident woman with a new hairstyle and fitted, designer clothes.

The circular space was light and airy beneath a high glass dome. She knew it had been built as The Montpellier Spa, the main attraction of the Victorian era Cheltenham.

She spotted Zivah, waving at her from the far side of the central bar, which had its own low-level roof from which green ivy was cascading down. She thought it looked like an English version of a Caribbean beach bar.

Smiling to herself, she pushed past a large palm in a pot and approached her sister's table.

"Sis, you got away. Is Gilly coping?" asked Zivah.

"I think she's got the hang of it."

"How's my kitchen?" called her mother from the far side of the table. She was sitting next to Keya and Zivah's younger sister, Maitri, who was bright and as excitable as the schoolgirl she was, or at least had been until she'd left school the previous month after completing her final set of public exams.

"Um ..."

"Don't worry, I'll soon have it back in shape next week."

Relieved, Keya saw her mum smile and turn to Keya's aunt as she said, "And last week we served thirty people just for lunch ..."

Keya turned back to Zivah, who whispered, "I ordered for you. I hope that's OK, but my appointment at Laboni's is at half past two."

"Thanks, and sorry I'm late."

"I expected it, and I understand how hard it is to leave the cafe to someone else. I nearly called in yesterday to check you were OK, but Ira wouldn't let me."

Ira, Zivah's maid of honour turned round and smiled at Keya in a superior way.

Keya smiled back and said, "Good job, Ira. Zivah should be enjoying the build up to her wedding and not worrying about the cafe."

Touching her neck, Ira's smile faded, and Keya left her looking confused.

"Keya," called her twin cousins. "Come and sit with us. We're fed up with baby talk, and we want to hear more about your fabulous cafe. Both your Amma and Zivah are so excited about working there."

Keya sat down on a curved red leather bench, with a large fresco of a white horse painted on the wall behind her, and enjoyed her cousins' company as she ate a deliciously light cheese and basil soufflé, followed by a fragrant coconut, vegetable curry with jasmine rice.

At a quarter past two, Zivah stood up and said, "Thank you all so much for joining me today. Please don't worry about the bill. I'll sort that out and don't rush home. But I do need to leave to have my mehendi done for tomorrow."

Keya remembered when Zivah had chosen the henna mehendi design for her hands and arms, and it seemed such a long time ago. After a clash at the original wedding venue, Zivah had moved both her wedding date and venue.

"Keya," Zivah called, shaking her out of her introspection.

Ira and Maitri were already standing beside Zivah.

"Now remember girls," Keya's mum called, "we are hosting the Ganesh Puja this evening, so don't be late back. There is much work to do."

CHAPTER SEVEN

Keya yawned, stretched, and felt the carpeted floor of Zivah's bedroom on which she'd slept on a narrow mattress.

She smiled. Today was Zivah's wedding and the sun was already illuminating her sister's colourful pink silk curtains, with yellow and blue patterns.

Let's hope it stays fine, she thought, as the ceremony was in the garden of Windrush Hall, the home of former rock star, Jay Newton.

Technically, the marriage proceedings had started the evening before, as her parents had hosted the traditional Hindu ceremony of Ganesh Puja.

"Morning," Zivah yawned, looking down at Keya from the same bed she'd had since she was a child. Zivah had decorated it with garlands of colourful tassels, some with small bells hanging from them, and a pink feathery dream catcher was hanging above the bed. "Did you sleep OK?" she asked.

"Actually, I did," Keya replied. "But I was tired. The Ganesh Puja was full on."

"Didn't Amma do a wonderful job? All those fabulous red flowers, and the decoration of Lord Ganesh's statue."

"She did. And she's so proud of you." Every Hindu marriage ceremony began by invoking Lord Ganesh, the Elephant God of

Hindus. "And you've already overcome so many obstacles, but I think that's why Amma insisted we had the ceremony here, last night, so Lord Ganesh will bless you and today will proceed smoothly." Keya crossed her fingers.

"I hope so," Zivah yawned again. "When are we going to Windrush Hall?"

"I'll drive you and Maitri over at half past nine. Amma and Appa can come later, but I bet they don't. Amma will want to check everything is in place for the ceremony, and she's bound to start rearranging flowers."

"True," Zivah said, sitting up on the side of her bed. She laughed happily. "Can you believe I'm finally getting married?"

Keya entered the music room, which overlooked the garden at the back of Windrush Hall. The French windows were open, and she could hear the sounds of drumming and singing floating through them.

"Is that the groom and his family arriving?" asked the shaven-headed Jay Newton. He'd entered into the spirit of the wedding and was wearing a long midnight-blue silk jacket.

"Yes," Zivah squeaked, as she grasped Keya's arm. "This is really happening," she added excitedly.

"I know," Keya smiled back. She was wearing a short, fitted, pale turquoise-blue jacket with delicate organza half sleeves over a floating floor-length skirt. Elegant gold embroidery decorated her jacket, and the skirt had ribbons and ruffles around the hem. Zivah had chosen the gorgeous outfit, and she felt very … feminine.

"Who's the tall, young guy with you?" whispered one of her twin cousins. "He can't keep his eyes off you."

Keya smiled at Ryan, who looked as self-conscious as she currently felt. He was wearing a long deep gold silk jacket over a customary pair of pyjama style trousers. Zivah had persuaded Keya to bring him as her plus one after they'd all worked together on a recent investigation.

He'd been fascinated by the prospect of a Hindu wedding, but now, standing with Keya's family, waiting for the groom's party to arrive, he looked out of place.

Keya turned back to her sister and holding her at arm's-length, considered her. Zivah had forgone a brightly coloured traditional wedding dress, instead choosing a wonderfully ornate ivory lehanga. The heavily gold embroidered top was cropped, revealing Zivah's narrow waist, and the full floor-length skirt was also covered in gold embroidery designs.

"Beautiful, inside and out," Keya marvelled.

Zivah drew her sister to her and hugged her.

"We should get ready," Ira said sharply. "The groom's party is on its way."

Zivah let go of Keya, who stepped back and whispered, "Good luck."

"What's happening?" asked Ryan, as Keya joined him beside the piano.

"This is the baraat. Aadi will be riding a horse ..."

"A horse?"

"Yes, it's part of the wedding tradition. A dhol band is playing the music, and the singing will be Aadi's friends and family. I think they were meeting at the lodge, at the top of the drive, and coming down it in procession to the front of the hall."

"I bet it looks impressive," Ryan said. "Singing and dancing down the drive, through the parkland, to this large Georgian house. And all those flower arrangements decorating the front steps leading up to the entrance."

"That's where the Pokhana will be held, when Mum and Dad welcome Aadi and his family."

With a sudden urge, Keya grabbed Ryan's hand. "Come on, let's go out through the kitchen. Then we can see the procession and watch the Pokhana."

Keya pulled Ryan through the house and out through the kitchen's side door into a courtyard. Dashing round the side of the house, they slowed to watch the approaching procession.

"Wow, what fun," Ryan enthused, "and Aadi looks very regal. And the horse even has a red plume on its head."

Keya laughed. "We love to show off, although Zivah has insisted the ceremony itself is more ... tasteful."

They watched as Aadi led the procession on his white horse. It had a red and gold rug with a matching cloth draped over its neck.

"The horse is very good, considering all the singing, and it doesn't seem bothered by people dancing around it."

"It'll be used to it," Keya called back as the volume increased and Aadi's friends and families swarmed round the horse and onto the drive in front of the hall. Two men continued to beat the drums they were carrying with their hands, and the guests in front of the house danced more energetically.

Keya looked up as her mum and dad stepped out of the hall's main entrance, followed by Maitri. Other members of the family jostled for a position on the top step as Amma and Appa walked slowly down towards the colourful wedding party.

The red-suited groom, who'd led the horse, helped Aadi dismount.

He smoothed down his jacket, before stepping forward to meet Keya's parents.

As Ryan had observed, two large arrangements of yellow, orange, and red flowers were positioned at the bottom of the stone steps. Other flowers adorned the steps leading up to the front door, where more flowers were arranged in an arch.

Amma laid a red cloth on the ground and, bare-footed, Aadi stepped onto it. The twin cousins descended the steps carrying a bowl and towel and they were preceded by Maitri carrying a pink and white garland of flowers.

"Come on," said Keya, grabbing Ryan's hand again. "Let's make sure we have good seats for the rest of the ceremony."

She led Ryan back past the kitchen door and through a stone arch into the garden.

The ceremony was being held at the far end where, fortuitously, Jay had erected a neo-classical circular stone temple, and landscaped the area looking out over the park.

The columned temple, with its wrought iron filigree domed roof, was being used as the Mandap for the main wedding ceremony, and two chairs had been placed inside it.

The roof and columns were beautifully decorated with pink and white flowers. Rows of chairs had been positioned for the wedding guests on either side of the gravel path which led through the garden to the temple.

"Here they come," cried Keya, pulling Ryan down the gravel path. As the wedding party rounded the corner, accompanied by more singing and the beating of drums, Keya found chairs in the second row for herself and Ryan.

Zivah only appeared, escorted by Amma's two brothers, when all the guests were seated and Aadi's family and friends had finally stopped singing.

"Why are those girls holding a cloth up in front of Aadi?" whispered Ryan.

"He's not allowed to see Zivah until she is inside the Mandap."

The ceremony was wonderful, beginning with an exchange of garlands between the couple, and Ryan was fascinated by the fire round which the couple walked four times while the priest, dressed in a white gown, chanted.

Zivah raced back to her chair, sitting down before Aadi, and Keya muttered, remembering the old saying for this particular wedding tradition, "First to sit, rules the house."

The ceremony continued, followed by at least half an hour of photographs. Ryan was shuffling restlessly in his chair when Zivah threw a handful of rice over her head, symbolising the repayment of all her parents had given her during her life, and the happy couple left the circular stone temple.

Zivah clasped Keya's hand, and then those of her other relatives as she symbolically said goodbye to them and her old life.

"Most brides are crying by this point, but Zivah looks delighted," said Keya. "Come on, let's join the party. You must be hungry."

Ryan stood up stiffly after sitting for so long, and replied, "I'm starving."

CHAPTER EIGHT

It was nearly eleven o'clock by the time Keya arrived at the Waterwheel Cafe on Friday morning, and she was feeling rather groggy.

It was times like this that she welcomed not drinking, as she knew from watching other people that a hangover made the morning after a party far worse.

And it had been a fun party. At least for her. She hoped Ryan had enjoyed himself despite all her older relatives asking him when he and Keya were getting married.

She'd warned him that they'd think he was her romantic partner, so he was able to answer them easily and politely with, "It's early days. We're just enjoying each other's company as friends."

She lifted the box of her mother's baking out of the car, wondering how, with the wedding and cooking for the Ganesh Puja the evening before it, Amma had had time to cook for the cafe. But her mother had been insistent.

A hum of voices greeted her when she entered the antique centre. One of the stallholders reached up and removed a vintage metal sign, advertising car oil, from a collection on the wall as Keya walked by.

"Morning," he said as she passed.

"Hiya," she replied, with less than her usual enthusiasm.

When she entered the cafe, Gilly turned to her with a bright smile and her even brighter, but today well controlled, orange curly hair.

"Keya! We weren't expecting you. I thought you were one of the customers. How was the wedding?" Gilly gushed.

"Amazing," Keya replied, smiling. "And so worth the wait. We held the ceremony outside in Jay's garden. And it was perfect."

"As was the weather. You were lucky."

"I know. How are things here?" Keya glanced past Gilly at the cafe, which was half full, and had a relaxed feel today.

"Aunt Beanie is thoroughly enjoying herself in the kitchen, but I hate to think what state it's in. But, encouraged by your mum, she keeps thinking up her own specials. Today's is a sandwich mix of chicken with mustard, tarragon, and slices of radish, served with crunchy iceberg lettuce. It's actually rather tasty."

"And Thomas?"

"This job is doing him the world of good. The students have taken him under their wing and he's now serving customers. See?"

Thomas was carrying a tray of drinks across to three ladies sitting beside the waterwheel window. He said something to the women, who laughed as he placed their order on the table. Keya followed his progress back to the serving counter and gasped, "Is that Norman?"

"Yes," chuckled Gilly. "Aunt Beanie instructed him to be here on Tuesday lunchtime to help cover for you. He wasn't keen on greeting or serving customers, but he loves that coffee machine. Taken to it like a duck to water."

"Oh good. I'll need someone who can work it after the students return to university."

"Hey!" Gilly jabbed Keya's arm playfully. "Don't go stealing my porter, even if he only works part-time."

Keya grimaced and rubbed her arm. Then she asked, "And have you been busy?"

"Not so much so that I haven't been able to chat to customers. Do you know, there are some who've been visiting the antique centre for years and I've never met them? Yesterday I started chatting to a couple who agreed to rent a small concession so they could sell their daughter's jewellery. They're helping her set up her own business."

"That's excellent news. And I'm glad the cafe is supporting the antique centre."

"Oh, it is. Exactly what we needed. Which reminds me. Can you do a special lunch for a coach party of visitors from Germany next Wednesday? Their budget is £10 per head, to include drinks."

"I'll need to think about it, and what staff will be here."

"Thomas can help, and let me know if you need me, too. And I'm sure Aunt Beanie will lend a hand." Gilly grinned at Keya.

"I better go and see Aunt Beanie, and sort out these cakes Mum gave me."

Keya crossed the cafe, smiling at customers and exchanging pleasantries with some of her regulars.

She stopped at the counter and said, "I hope you don't mind being drafted in to help, Norman."

Norman, in his late sixties, had a permanently tanned face, with broken veins from his years spent outdoors at Windrush Hall, where he had worked as estate manager and general handyman for the original owner, the Duke of Ditchford.

Aunt Beanie must have told him to be presentable for the cafe as his sandy hair was cut short and his greying beard neatly trimmed. "It's not bad working this huge machine. Rather cathartic, actually. Would you like anything?" Norman asked.

"Oh, I'd love a cup of tea."

"Which flavour?"

"Nothing too flowery. I think English Breakfast. Thanks. I'll just check on Aunt Beanie."

Keya opened the door to the kitchen. Aunt Beanie was frying bacon and something else was under the grill. She either didn't hear Keya, or she was ignoring her.

"Hiya," called Keya, but Aunt Beanie still didn't reply.

The older woman turned round, picked up a plate, and nearly dropped it. Startled, she cried, "Oh, Keya. Just a minute."

Placing the bacon in an open bun, the older woman added slices of tomato and a leaf of iceberg lettuce, before closing the bun and placing the plate on the hatch.

Then she removed an ear plug and explained, "I wanted to listen to podcasts and music, but Gilly complained I was disturbing the customers. So Norman bought me a pair of these."

She held up the blue plastic box into which she placed her ear pod. "I only wear one and usually I hear when people need me."

She hadn't heard Keya so either the music was loud, or she'd been concentrating on something and was distracted.

"The chicken," cried Aunt Beanie as she grabbed an oven mitt and yanked the tray out from under the grill. "It's OK. That was lucky." Placing the tray on a metal rack, she turned back to Keya and said, "My special sandwich fillings are going down well. Would you like to try today's?"

"Perhaps later, thanks. If you're OK in here, I'll go and get my tea, which Norman is making. Thanks for bringing him along to help."

"He needed something to do, and also to have a break from the auction house and antique centre. I don't like to say anything, but I do wonder if he's getting too old to be lugging heavy pieces of furniture around."

She lowered her voice and confided, "And I think he rather enjoys using that coffee machine. He keeps talking about becoming a professional barista. He was looking up courses on the internet when we got home yesterday evening."

"Oh, if he's interested in doing one of those, the company I rent the machine from run one-day workshops."

"Sounds perfect."

Thomas' voice called through the hatch. "Two bacon and egg rolls."

Keya left Aunt Beanie to prepare the order and re-joined Norman at the serving counter. As she sipped her tea gratefully, she told him about the barista courses.

"Sign me up," he replied gruffly. "That is, if you don't mind me helping out. It can get a bit lonely being the porter and," he lowered his voice, "I can't keep lifting heavy furniture forever."

Keya considered that for once, Norman and Aunt Beanie were in agreement.

New customers entered the cafe. Jonathan, who'd been in the previous Saturday, was holding the hand of his young son, Zaad. They were followed by Biljana, the nanny, and, no, it wasn't Jonathan's wife.

It was her older sister. But then it was Friday, and she remembered that Malika had a demanding job.

"Jonathan, shall we sit outside?" the older sister asked.

"No, it's too close to the river. But that group is leaving from one of the tables beside the waterwheel, Nadia."

Gilly stopped and turned to them. "If you'd like that table, can you give me a few minutes to prepare it?"

"Of course," Jonathan replied, and the group gathered beside the counter, next to Keya.

"I can't believe most of the toddler groups stop during the summer holidays," Jonathan complained.

"I guess most families go on holiday, and some will have older, school-age children at home," considered Nadia.

"I guess so."

Nadia held up her finger and Zaad grasped it. She said warmly, "I've never been keen on children. And, as you know, Xavier and I couldn't have them, but Zaad is a joy. You and Malika are so lucky."

"I know," Jonathan admitted, "I don't know what I'd do if anything happened to him. He's my world."

"Well, I'm happy to look after him this afternoon if you want to do some painting. Malika's right, you really should try to sell some of your work."

Jonathan shuffled his feet. "Thanks for the offer, and I am seeing a gallery owner tomorrow."

Jonathan turned to the nanny and said, "Are you OK looking after Zaad tomorrow morning? I'll be back by lunch."

Biljana nodded. "I'll ask Jason to pick me up a little later."

"Your table's ready," Gilly said, returning to the group.

As they followed her across to an empty table beside the waterwheel window, Keya put down her mug and opened the box her mother had given her.

She removed a plastic container and lifted the lid to reveal slices of almond and cardamom cake. Perfect to go with a cup of tea. Without thinking, she picked up a slice and bit into it.

CHAPTER NINE

On Saturday afternoon, Keya was serving in the cafe. She placed a fruit scone in front of a customer, together with a small white ramekin of clotted cream, and another of Norman's homemade raspberry jam.

She felt her phone vibrate in her pocket. Smiling at the customer, she turned and walked towards the outside door, removing her phone from her pocket and, without checking the caller ID, she answered, "Hello."

"Keya."

She was immediately alert. Ryan's voice was hushed and full of anxiety.

"What's happened?" she asked, stepping outside, and walking towards the steps leading down to the river.

"A young boy's been kidnapped. I thought you ought to know. Just in case you're brought into the investigation."

"Thanks, Ryan. But how do you know it's a kidnapping? Couldn't the boy have just wandered off or run away?"

"He's too young to run away and, shortly after he disappeared, a ransom note was left at the family's house."

"Which means whoever took him knows where he lives. And where is that?"

"Cedar Lane. Near the football club in Fairford."

This was personal then. Ryan lived in a cottage adjoining the main farmhouse where Aunt Beanie and Norman lived, at Meadowbank Farm, on the edge of the small town of Fairford.

Ryan continued, "The boy was out with his nanny this morning and when his father, Jonathan, returned home at lunchtime, the ransom letter was waiting for him."

Keya felt an uneasy churning in her tummy as she asked, "And the mother?"

"Malika. She was working this morning. She seemed calm enough when one of our colleagues collected her from a client's house, but she became hysterical when she saw the ransom note. She was crying and asking how did they know, and how we can be sure it's from the person who took her son."

Keya swallowed, a sour taste in her mouth. She hesitated before asking, "Is the boy a toddler called Zaad?"

"Yes. But how did you know that?" Ryan asked, sounding incredulous.

"Because they're customers at the cafe. In fact, they were here yesterday. Not the wife. She was working. But the boy, his father, and the nanny. And the mother's older sister."

"That's another thing," Ryan added. "Nadia, the sister, was here when Jonathan went out this morning, but she's also disappeared. Packed up her clothes and everything."

"Do you think she took Zaad?" Keya remembered the conversation she'd overheard the previous day and how Nadia had amazed herself by becoming attached to the little boy.

If she remembered correctly, Nadia had recently left her husband, and she did say something about them not being able to have children.

Into the phone she said, "But if Nadia took Zaad, why the ransom note?"

"Chief Inspector Greg's been questioning that, too."

"Is he there?" asked Keya in surprise.

"He is, but he's very agitated. As you know, he's due to go on holiday tomorrow with his family."

"And he'll be in big trouble if he puts work first again," Keya added. "Is there anything I can do?"

"I'm not sure. I'd say come over, but it's not my place to tell you that. But perhaps you can explain to Aunt Beanie and Norman what's happened. Some of the Fairford residents have already taken it upon themselves to start searching for Zaad."

Keya finished her call and closed her eyes against the afternoon sun. Just when she thought all was well in the world, a child went missing.

"Table 12 needs serving, and should I put up the closed sign?" she heard Gilly ask. "New customers are still arriving."

Keya sighed. She couldn't even stop to think for a minute.

"What is it?" Gilly asked, stepping closer.

Keya opened her eyes and said, "A toddler's missing. A little boy who was here yesterday. He was so excited by the waterwheel."

"No," gasped Gilly. "Do you know what's happened to him?'

Gilly told her the gist of Ryan's call. It was bound to be all over the local, and perhaps national, evening news.

"You better tell Aunt Beanie and Norman. I'll serve table 12 and close the cafe."

"Thanks," Keya said, as they both turned and walked back inside.

"We have to help," cried Aunt Beanie, when Keya finished telling her and Norman about the missing boy.

"I'll drive us around Fairford this evening," Norman suggested. "Do you know where he went missing from?"

"No, I forgot to ask." Keya's phone pinged, and she checked her messages. "Ryan has sent me a press release. Apparently, Zaad and his nanny were at The Walnut Tree Playing Field this morning."

"I know it," interrupted Aunt Beanie. "It's at the top end of the town. Lots of kids play there."

Still reading the press release, Keya confirmed, "That's where he disappeared from. A special enclosed play area for toddlers."

"Under the nose of his nanny?" Aunt Beanie commented, in an I-don't-quite-believe-it voice.

"Have they mentioned the ransom note?" Norman asked.

"No, all it says is that the police are appealing to witnesses."

"You hear that, Beanie? Don't go blurting about ransom notes and kidnapping this evening in town. Remember, this is only about a missing boy for the moment."

"But what's the point of searching for him, if he's been kidnaped?"

Keya sighed. "I guess in case it's a hoax, and he's just wandered off, or if anyone finds any evidence of where he's gone. It says in the press release he took his toy rabbit with him."

Aunt Beanie's face fell. "Poor little mite."

CHAPTER TEN

Keya hung round close to the tables where two sets of customers remained in the cafe. Why wouldn't they go home? It was after half-past five on Saturday afternoon.

Aunt Beanie and Norman had already left, and they'd said they would go straight into Fairford to help search for Zaad.

"Keya," Gilly whispered.

"Yes."

Gilly gestured with her hand for Keya to approach her. When Keya was close to her, Gilly said, "You're making those people uncomfortable. Why don't you go, and I'll close up? I have to check the antique centre anyway, and I can see you're anxious to leave."

"Thanks," Keya replied gratefully. "It's this missing boy. It feels personal. I guess because I know the family, and after my last case …" Even though the missing person that time had been a fully grown woman.

Gilly laid a hand on Keya's arm and consoled her. "I understand. You may be running your own cafe now but, in your heart, you're still a police officer."

Keya drew her lips together and nodded. "Something like that."

Keya grabbed her bag and entered the antique centre, which was ghostly quiet as she wandered through it. She knew it would be full of chattering voices the next day.

Just as the cafe would. But for the first time, she wasn't looking forward to coming to her café. The missing boy must be affecting her mood.

Despite not being formally told about the case, or asked to attend, Keya couldn't help driving straight to Cedar Lane, Fairford. And she wasn't the only one making her way along the narrow lane.

She joined a queue of cars moving more slowly than the surrounding people. The people were mostly men, dressed in red football shirts with white vertical stripes.

Of course. There must be a football match on, although it was an early start to the season.

She had no trouble finding the home of the missing boy, as Ryan was on duty at the entrance.

Keya indicated and slowly pushed her way through the crowd of football supporters. "I didn't realise Fairford Football Club had such a following," she said to Ryan, after lowering her car window.

"It's the first match of the season, and an important one. The FA Cup extra preliminary round."

Keya had heard of the FA cup, but only when top teams like Liverpool or Manchester United were involved.

She'd occasionally heard of the big league teams being beaten by those from lower divisions, and she guessed the tournament must start at the town level.

"I'd park at this end," Ryan suggested. "Out of the way."

Keya did as Ryan suggested and then walked back to him across a neat gravel drive.

The house, with cream painted walls and a black slate roof, looked new and was built back from the road, probably in a field or part of the garden of the large, detached house she could just see over the tall hedge.

Ryan was watching the steady stream of football supporters with an interested expression.

"I thought you supported another team, with blue soccer kit," Keya said when she joined him at the entrance.

"I do. Cheltenham Town. But Fairford Town is my local team, and

Norman and I attended a few matches last season. They're plucky, and I'd prefer to be watching the game tonight, rather than worrying about a small boy."

One of the supporters stepped forward and thrust an envelope at Keya.

Surprised, she let it fall to the ground.

"Hey!" cried Ryan, running into the lane. "Where did you get that?"

One of the red-shirted football fans called back, "From a bloke at the end of the lane wearing a baseball cap."

Keya looked towards the voice, but the fans merged together.

Ryan turned and shook his head.

Realising that the envelope might be from the kidnapper, Keya did not pick it up. It was a long, plain white envelope like any you'd buy at a shop or supermarket. And it wasn't addressed to anyone.

"Here," Ryan said.

She turned and took the blue plastic gloves he held out, together with a transparent evidence bag. Wearing the gloves, she picked up the envelope, placing it in the bag.

"I better stay here," Ryan said. "Can you take it to the chief inspector?"

Gravel crunched under Keya's feet as she strode towards the entrance to the single-storey house holding the evidence bag and still wearing the plastic gloves.

She passed through the entrance porch, where several coats were hanging neatly from a coat rail above a wooden shoe rack with a cushion seat, and into a large kitchen dining area.

Someone she didn't recognise was sitting at the central L-shaped island tapping on a computer.

She heard voices, and a worried-looking Chief Inspector Greg emerged from a door to her left.

He stopped pulling at his chin when he saw her and asked, "Keya? What are you doing here? And what is that?"

Holding up the evidence bag, Keya told him how an unknown football fan had thrust it at her. "And all we know about the person who gave it to him is that it was a man, and he was wearing a baseball cap."

"Which doesn't narrow it down in the slightest."

A second door into the kitchen opened, opposite Keya, and Malika appeared, her eyes bloodshot. Jonathan was behind her, pale-faced.

"Something's happened, hasn't it?" Jonathan said.

"Yes." Inspector Greg turned to the couple. "We're received another note."

Malika cried, "What does it say?"

"We don't know." The chief inspector held out his hand and Keya gave him the evidence bag, which he carried back into the room behind the kitchen.

"You're from the cafe at the antique centre, aren't you?" Malika sniffed. "Why did someone give you the envelope?" Her eyes narrowed.

As Keya peeled off her gloves, she replied, "I do run the cafe, and I've seen you all there, but I'm also a part-time police officer. Full-time until recently. And I was standing with the constable at the entrance to your drive when we were given the envelope."

Jonathan stepped forward and asked, "By whom?"

"Sorry," said Keya. "It was one of the football supporters who merged back into the crowd going to the match. But he was only the courier, and not involved in Zaad's disappearance."

Jonathan's eye widened. "Of course. It's the FA cup qualifier. I have tickets for this evening's game."

Chief Inspector Greg reappeared, holding a crisp A4 sheet of paper. "The note says, "Your boy is safe. Make sure you have the £48,000 ready by tomorrow morning. Await further instructions."

Malika paled and grabbed hold of the central island.

"Tomorrow," gasped Jonathan. "But by tomorrow he might be …"

"Mr Bartlett," Inspector Sue interrupted, entering the kitchen. "It is in the kidnapper's best interest to look after Zaad."

"But I've never spent a night apart from him."

"Of course you haven't," snapped Malika. "You won't even let me take him to visit my parents when I have a few days' holiday. But it's all right to take him to yours when I'm working."

"It's OK, Mrs Bartlett," Inspector Sue tried to placate her. "This is an extremely stressful time. Let's go back to the snug so you can show me some more photos of Zaad."

Inspector Sue led Malika away as Jonathan demanded, "So that's it? We just have to wait until tomorrow?"

"No, that's not all," Chief Inspector Greg responded in a strained voice.

"We have officers and local residents out looking for Zaad. And my team are checking CCTV cameras, not that there are many in Fairford, and local media feeds from people at and around the park today. I promise that we'll do everything we can to get Zaad back."

The chief inspector halted and swallowed. "But I do think you should be prepared to pay the ransom, if you can."

Jonathan nodded. "I agree, but Malika has control of the account, and she's refusing to authorise the money withdrawal. But Sue has spoken to the bank, and they are waiting for her instruction."

"Let's speak to her again," Inspector Greg said. "We should at least have the money ready to hand over, if you agree that's what we should do."

"I do. I'd give anything to bring Zaad home." Jonathan opened the door opposite Keya and left the kitchen.

Chief Inspector Greg turned to Keya and sighed, "I hate cases with missing children."

CHAPTER ELEVEN

Keya and Chief Inspector Greg stood in the kitchen of the Bartletts' house in Cedar Lane, Fairford.

The man sitting on a stool at the central island looked up and said, "I've been through all the footage I can find on social media from the park this morning. I can confirm Zaad was playing in the fenced off section of the playground and his nanny, Biljana, was with him. In the last photo I've found of them both, the boy is walking along a platform on the wooden climbing frame and the nanny is talking to another woman at the roundabout in the corner."

"And what time was that photo taken?"

"Five past eleven."

"And the nanny called us thirty-five minutes later."

"Yes, sir."

"So why the delay?" asked Chief Inspector Greg.

Keya cleared her throat. "If I may, sir. The boy might not have gone missing straight away, and then Biljana would need to notice he wasn't there. The first thing I'd do is search the playground, and the wider area surrounding it, and ask other parents if they'd seen Zaad. And phoning us might not have been her first response. I'm guessing by her name, and her accent, that she's East European?"

"Bulgarian," confirmed the chief inspector. "And I agree with all you've said. But she didn't call either of the boy's parents."

"Someone else?" suggested Keya.

"Sergeant Ross." Chief Inspector Greg addressed the man seated at the island.

"Yes, sir."

"Find the nanny's phone and see who she contacted between 11 o'clock and midday."

"Yes, sir." Sergeant Ross left the kitchen.

"So Sergeant Varma. I didn't think you were on duty, so what are you doing here?"

"With my role, I'm always on duty to a certain extent."

"You and me both," Chief Inspector Greg accepted in a resigned tone.

"And I know the family."

Chief Inspector Greg tilted his head as he looked at her.

"That is, they've visited my cafe. In fact, the father and the boy, with the nanny and the wife's older sister, came in yesterday. It makes it feel rather personal."

"Feeling is a bad habit in our job," acknowledged the chief inspector. He walked across to the kettle and switched it on.

As it hummed into life, the chief inspector asked, "So what's your impression of the family?"

Keya walked across to the counter, not wanting Zaad's parents to overhear her response, even though the door to the next room was closed.

"Malika works hard, too hard, I'd say. And she regrets the time she can't spend with her son. And she resents Jonathan, who doesn't appear to contribute financially to the family, but is happy to spend money on flash cars to keep up with the yummy mummies at the toddler groups he takes Zaad to."

"So it's not all happy families then," the chief inspector said dryly as he reached up to a shelf and removed two cups.

"What families are?"

Chief Inspector Greg flinched before picking up the jar of coffee and unscrewing the lid.

"I'd say there are issues between them in terms of work, time, and finances," Keya concluded.

"Which might be why Mrs Bartlett isn't keen to pay the ransom money." The chief inspector handed Keya a mug of black coffee.

"But they do have it, don't they?" Keya remembered the Bartletts talking about a similar sum for a new car.

"Yes, and the bank is willing to co-operate. This kidnapper is not sophisticated, or perhaps he's just pragmatic as he's asked for the money in used ten and twenty-pound notes."

"That'll be a lot of notes." Keya sipped the coffee. While she rarely drank it in the evening, and certainly not black, she welcomed its bitter taste.

"Not as many as you might think. They'll all fit into an overnight bag."

Sergeant Ross reappeared carrying a mobile phone in a case with a floral design. He said, "Biljana was not happy to hand this over, and I didn't mean to scare her when I said it was a police matter, but she is upset."

Keya suggested, "Why don't I speak to her while Sergeant Ross checks her phone?"

Chief Inspector Greg nodded and, taking this as consent, Keya made herself and Biljana a cup of tea - which she knew was a very English thing to do - and left the kitchen by the door Sergeant Ross had used.

She entered a corridor. On the left she passed a utility room, and she heard voices behind the door on her right, which she judged to be the room the Bartletts and Inspector Sue were using. As Sergeant Ross hadn't entered that room, Biljana must be elsewhere in the house.

She could hear soft music behind the next door on her left, so she knocked on it.

"Yes," she heard Biljana's accented voice say.

"I thought you might like a cup of tea."

The door opened a fraction and Biljana's tear-stained face stared out at her.

Keya held up a mug, and the door opened wider. Taking her tea, Biljana turned and walked across the small room to a single bed pushed against the wall and sat down. Keya followed her inside.

The room was compact, with a pine wardrobe behind the door and a matching chest of drawers against the wall opposite the bed. A wicker chair was covered with clothes, so Keya remained standing, cradling her own mug of tea. She sipped it. Far more refreshing than black coffee.

"Thank you," whispered Biljana. She also sipped her tea before looking up and studying Keya. "Why are you here? You work in the cafe with the big wheel, don't you?"

Keya smiled and replied, "I do. But I'm also a police officer. I came to see if I could help with the search for Zaad."

"They blame me, you know. Jonathan and Malika. Especially Jonathan. I thought he was going to hit me when I came back without Zaad. But I only took my eyes off him for a moment, I swear. And I looked everywhere. And I asked my friends and other mums at the playground. But none of them see Zaad."

"Nobody should blame you," Keya sympathised. "And if you don't feel safe staying here, we could find you somewhere else to spend the night. But until Zaad returns, we do need to keep you under observation."

"You see. You blame me, too."

"No. I don't," Keya replied evenly. "But this is a difficult and delicate situation. Our priority is finding Zaad and bringing him safely home."

Biljana sniffed. "I want that too. Poor Zaad. He must be so scared."

"I'm sure you've been over this many times, but can you tell me what happened at the park? Just in case you think of something new."

Biljana sighed. "Both Jonathan and Malika go out this morning and as it's sunny day I take Zaad to The Walnut Tree Playing Field."

"Is that where you normally go?" questioned Keya.

"Sometimes, although there is smaller playground at the end of Manor Close. But Malika suggest The Walnut Tree, and today there is pop-up cafe."

"OK, so you left for the playground at?"

"Just after nine o'clock, when Jonathan go out."

"And you played until?"

"Just after 10. I met my friend Ana, and Kiera, the little girl she looks after, and we had coffee and the kids ice creams at the cafe."

"And who paid?"

"I did, with the £20 Malika gave me." She reached into her pocket and removed some coins, which she held out. "I not steal. Here is the change. I not able to give it back to Malika."

"Would you like me to?" Keya asked softly.

Biljana nodded.

Keya took the money. "So after coffee, you and Ana took the kids to the enclosed playground?" Keya suggested.

"Yes. Keira wanted to be pushed on the roundabout but Zaad, he love the climbing frame. I promise, I only turn my back for short time to help Ana secure Keira on the seat. Then I turn back to Zaad, but he was gone."

"And you didn't hear him shout, or cry out?"

"No, and neither did Ana."

"And nobody in the play area saw him with another adult, or even a child."

"No. Nobody see anything. But how could he just disappear?" Biljana's voice became shrill.

"I don't know." Keya leaned against the pine wardrobe and waited for Biljana to compose herself. Then she asked, "Was the park busy?"

"Oh yes. There were other children in the enclosure and bigger children using the zip slide, swings, and large climbing frame outside. Older kids were messing around by the table tennis table and others were playing football."

The park being busy probably made it easier for Zaad's abductor to slip away, Keya thought to herself.

"OK, so what did you do when you realised Zaad was missing?"

"I said. I look for him. All over. And I ask big children. But they not see him."

"And after that?"

"I know I get the blame. I get into trouble for losing Zaad. So I call Jason."

"Is that your boyfriend?"

"Yes. He's good to me, although he scares other people."

Keya remembered the shaven-headed man with tattoos who'd met Biljana in the cafe. "And what did he tell you to do?" she asked.

"Call the police."

CHAPTER TWELVE

Keya left Biljana in her bedroom. The nanny was still upset though not hysterical, but Keya doubted she'd sleep much, if at all, that night as she worried about her missing charge.

"What do you think?" Chief Inspector Greg whispered when she returned to the kitchen.

"About?"

"About the nanny? Was she involved in the abduction? She's the obvious person to point the finger at."

"I don't think she had anything to do with it. Not unless she's an exceptionally good actress. And living in this brand-new house, with new electrical appliances and furnishings, wouldn't she just ask if she wanted more money?"

"£48,000 is probably a lot to someone like her."

"It's also a very precise figure," Keya observed.

Chief Inspector Greg held eye contact with Keya as he revealed, "And it happens to be the exact amount that's in the account Jonathan says Malika has access to. Which brings me back to Biljana."

"Because she might have overheard them arguing about it, just as I did in the cafe last week? And for that matter, the people sitting near their table. And if Jonathan raised it then, how many other times has he mentioned it in public?"

"I see what you mean. So the amount of the ransom doesn't really help us?"

"Not at the moment," Keya agreed. "Any update on paying it?"

"Not that I've been informed."

"Sir?"

"Yes, Sergeant Ross."

"Social Media is exploding with news of the missing boy. Including videos of the search parties in Fairford."

Keya heard a voice from the computer say something about civic duty. It sounded very much like Aunt Beanie.

"Inspector Unwin and your media team will have a busy night," the chief inspector said to Sergeant Ross.

"They're on their way now."

"Then I better clear my stuff out of the living room." As the chief inspector strode across the kitchen, the door of the room where the Bartletts were opened, and Inspector Sue emerged. "Sir?"

The chief inspector stopped and turned to her.

"Malika has agreed to approve the withdrawal of the money. She's speaking to the bank now."

Chief Inspector Greg drew his lips together, looking glum, and nodded his head. "I think that's for the best."

Through the open door, Keya heard Malika's strained voice say, "Yes, used £10 and £20 notes."

"They'll courier the money to us first thing in the morning," Inspector Sue said as she joined Keya.

Chief Inspector Greg entered what Keya presumed was the living room and closed the door behind him.

"And if we have to pay more, can I access any of my other accounts?" Malika asked, still speaking to her bank manager.

"Let's hope we don't get further demands, but it can happen," Inspector Sue acknowledged.

"Then do that. Draw them all down into my main account." Malika sounded stronger and more resolute as she continued her discussion with the bank.

"I'm sure the bank can make an exception on the penalties, due to the circumstances. And hopefully I won't need any more money and I can reinvest it. But I could aways move it elsewhere."

Inspector Sue raised her eyebrows at Keya, as they listened to Malika's phone conversation.

"Good, I'm pleased we've come to an understanding. The ransom money will be here by six o'clock tomorrow morning, and the money from my other accounts moved to my main account, in case I need quick access to it. Thank you."

"I'm not sure what else we can do tonight," Inspector Sue said to Keya. "It's a waiting game now, so you might as well go home."

"And tomorrow morning?"

"That rather depends on the chief inspector. I know he'll want to be here for the handover, but he should be driving to the Lake District."

"Can't we handle this? After all, haven't you dealt with other kidnap cases?" Keya asked Inspector Sue.

"I have, but you know how he is. He's responsible for the case, so he wants to be here."

"But surely he moved to Cirencester so that he didn't have to be responsible for such cases?"

"You're right, I did," agreed the chief inspector as he returned to the kitchen carrying a leather briefcase.

"Which is why, despite deep reservations over his empathy and compassion, I'm handing this case over to Inspector Evans. I know you will look after the Bartletts Sue, while the inspector gets on with the police work."

"So you are going away with your family?" Keya asked.

"If this all goes wrong, the press will roast me for leaving the case. But, at the moment, I'm more worried about the grilling my wife will give me if I don't. She's threatened to stay up north with her family and not bring the children back if they go without me."

"Ouch," Keya muttered.

"That's one way of putting it." Chief Inspector Greg cleared his throat. "I've spoken to Inspector Evans, and we've agreed he'll take over tomorrow morning at six."

"The money is due here then, sir."

"You better make it a quarter to," said the chief inspector, looking at Keya.

"Yes, sir." Clearly Inspector Evans' appointment to the case included her presence.

"Since Inspector Unwin is on his way, and I presume you are staying here tonight, Sue?"

"Yes, sir. I always carry an overnight bag and a blow-up mattress in my car. I'll sleep in the snug and be on hand for the family."

"Then Keya, we might as well go home. And can you drop Constable Jenkins off? I think he lives near here. I'll have someone else stand guard at the gate tonight, especially when the football match ends."

"Fairford Town is two one down," Sergeant Ross called.

"More bad news for the town," muttered the chief inspector as he walked towards the front door. He stopped, turned round, and said, "Good luck, everyone."

"Enjoy your holiday, sir. And don't spend all your time on your phone or glued to the news. Go out cycling or canoeing with your kids. You'll never get these years with them back. And before you know it, they've grown up and left. Or at least, they do their own thing and don't want to be seen with their parents anymore."

The chief inspector smiled glumly. "I will, Sue. This is my second chance to keep my family. And I know I mustn't waste it."

CHAPTER THIRTEEN

"I better go too," Keya said, looking round the Bartletts' kitchen, "since it's going to be an early start."

"Night, and I hope you get some sleep," said Inspector Sue.

"You, too."

Keya's phone rang as she stepped out of the front door of the house. It was her boss, Inspector Evans.

"Evening, sir."

"Rum business this," Inspector Evans remarked. "A missing boy nobody saw leave a busy park, and a not particularly eye-watering ransom demand. I believe you're at the house. Is it an inside job?"

"You mean the nanny, Biljana? No, I don't think so, sir."

"We'll see. I understand the money's arriving at six in the morning. We better be there, and young Constable Jenkins, too."

"I'll let him know," said Keya as she walked across the gravel to the entrance of the property.

"Let's just hope the boy is returned when the ransom is paid, or we'll all be in hot water."

Not wanting to prolong the inspector's proclamations of doom, Keya said, "I'll see you in the morning, sir," and ended the call.

"Who was that?" Ryan asked.

"Inspector Evans, and he sounds far from happy about taking over this case."

"So the chief inspector is going on holiday. I saw him leave, but he just waved at me."

"For him, it's more than losing one child, it's his whole family. What choice does he have? And while we all know Inspector Evans isn't the most sympathetic of characters, he'll make sure every stone is unturned in the search for missing Zaad. Luckily, Inspector Sue is great with families."

"Where does that leave us?" asked Ryan.

"Off duty, but with an early start. We have to be here by the time the money is delivered, so before six."

Ryan groaned. "I'm supposed to be taking Mum out tomorrow to visit a country house and garden, and Aunt Beanie and Norman were joining us for lunch."

"You might still be able to make lunch," Keya replied, "if Zaad is returned in exchange for the money. Come on, here comes your replacement."

They stepped back as a police car driven by a young constable from Cirencester Police Station turned into the drive. He waved at them both.

Close by, they heard loud cheering. Ryan immediately checked his phone and smiled. "Fairford Town has scored an equaliser. And there's only five minutes left in the match."

"Then we better get out of here. I'll drop you home."

Keya and Ryan left Cedar Lane before the football supporters and Keya drove into the centre of the small town, past St. Mary's Church and across the stone bridge over the River Coln.

Keya still felt strange turning into the broken concrete yard of Meadowbank Farm and not meeting up with her friend Dotty, who had lived in the cottage adjacent to the main farmhouse for over a year, where Ryan now lived.

"You're thinking of Dotty, aren't you?" Ryan asked as they parked in front of the gates leading to his silver-grey front door.

"Yes, do you think she'll ever come back?"

"Her stuff's still in the cottage, so she'll have to return some time to sort it out."

An old, battered Land Rover Defender drew up alongside them and Norman and Aunt Beanie climbed out.

Aunt Beanie tapped on Keya's window and asked, "Are you coming in for supper?"

"You know she only wants an update on the case," Ryan said.

"I do, but she might also have info for us." Keya and Ryan climbed out of her little Polo and followed Aunt Beanie into the farmhouse.

Norman headed across the yard, no doubt to feed Buttercup, his Jersey cow, and Agatha, Aunt Beanie's Berkshire pig.

"Come in, come in," Aunt Beanie invited as Keya and Ryan hovered in the doorway to the large, comfortable, and familiar kitchen. It was still light outside, and Keya could see tall purple and white delphiniums through the full height windows at the far end, overlooking the garden and meadow beyond.

"Tea, Keya? And for you, Ryan? Or something stronger?"

"I think I'll have a beer," said Ryan, opening the fridge.

"Tea for me, please," Keya replied.

"And I brought home a vegetarian quiche from the cafe, which has been started but didn't look as if it would last until tomorrow," Aunt Beanie said. "And I've plenty of salad items in the fridge. Why don't you prepare something, Keya? I'll be back in a minute."

Keya found lettuce, cucumber, an orange pepper, and some cherry tomatoes and started making the salad.

Aunt Beanie returned with a handful of herbs, including chives, basil, and thyme, which she chopped up and added to the salad.

"I presume you didn't find Zaad," Keya said, slicing a cherry tomato in half.

"No, and there was a good crowd out. We must have covered every inch of The Walnut Tree Playing Field, but there was no sign of him. Do the police have any updates on his whereabouts?"

"No, we've no more idea than you. But we are expecting an exchange tomorrow, when the ransom money is paid, although keep that to yourself."

"People on the search were muttering about a kidnapping," Aunt Beanie remarked. "They said the Bartletts had been throwing their money around buying that new, over-priced house on Cedar Lane and filling it with state-of-the-art electronics and electrical items."

“And what did they say about the Bartletts themselves?” Keya asked.

“Pass me a baking tray will you, Ryan?”

Aunt Beanie requested, before replying, “Nobody’s seen much of the wife. She has a high-powered job and makes all the money. I think he’s a bit of a layabout. Calls himself an artist, but he’s never exhibited anything locally.

“Although, if it’s who I’m thinking of, I once saw some decent portrait pencil sketches of his. But now he likes to hang out with the trendy crowd of yummy mummies in their 4x4s, and doesn’t have much time for townsfolk.”

“I had a similar impression,” Keya agreed. “But he is genuinely upset about his missing son.”

“Who wouldn’t be? It’s a terrible thing to happen.” Aunt Beanie glanced at Keya’s finished salad. “Splendid. Put it on the table and Ryan can put out the cutlery and crockery. The quiche will be another ten minutes.”

CHAPTER FOURTEEN

The following morning, Keya yawned as she turned into the yard at Meadowbank Farm. Even though it was twenty to six in the morning, it was already light.

She'd driven carefully along the narrow lanes, swerving twice to miss young rabbits. Clearly the wild animals, accustomed to the roads being empty at such an early hour, were used to running about on them.

Ryan appeared, also yawning, as he pulled on his police jacket while gripping a piece of toast between his teeth.

He slid into the passenger seat without speaking and started to munch his toast.

"Morning," Keya said cheerfully as she reversed the car. She drove steadily through the sleeping town, pulling into the Bartletts' drive at ten to six.

Inspector Evans was waiting for them. "Good timing. Mrs Bartlett is in the kitchen, waiting to sign for the money and her husband is still asleep. We thought it best to leave him, as it could be another long day."

"Did Malika get any sleep?" asked Keya.

"Some. Sue said something about sleeping tablets, which was probably a sensible idea, given the circumstances. I haven't seen the nanny, but Sue has been keeping an eye on her too, and she took her some supper last night.

"The nanny's refused to come out of her room, but that's not surprising considering Inspector Onion and his media team tried to take over the kitchen and living room."

Keya rolled her eyes at Ryan who grinned. Even though Nick Unwin was now an inspector, and the same rank as Inspector Evans, the older police officer still insisted on calling Nick by the derogatory nickname he'd been given when working at Cirencester Police Station.

"Here we are," declared Inspector Evans.

A dark blue van, with the name of a secure courier service painted on the side, turned into the property. Both the driver and his companion wore protective helmets, although the driver had raised his transparent visor.

"Constable, please ask Mrs Bartlett to join us," the inspector instructed Ryan.

A minute later, Malika, wearing a pink dressing gown, and a pair of fluffy slippers on her feet, emerged from the house. She was accompanied by Inspector Sue who looked remarkably fresh in a different floral dress from the one she'd worn the day before.

The man in the passenger seat climbed out of the van and approached the assembled group. "Which of you is Mrs Malika Bartlett?" he asked.

"I am," replied Malika in a clear, calm voice.

"And I can vouch for her," said Inspector Evans, reaching into the inside pocket of his brown suit jacket and removing his warrant card. "Inspector Evans."

"Very good, sir." The courier handed Malika an electronic tablet and said, "Please sign here."

Malika used her finger to sign the tablet's screen. The courier waited and then nodded before returning to the van and standing beside it. A small hatch door opened, and he removed a black metal case. Holding it by its handle, he carried the case back to the group, depositing it on the gravel beside Malika.

"The bank will email you the passcode to open this."

Keya noticed that the case had a large yellow and red sticker on the side and the words 'Warning. Armed with Glue Destruction System'.

Malika better enter the correct password, or all the money would be destroyed.

"Thank you." Malika said, staring at the case.

"Constable, will you do the honours?" Inspector Evans looked at Ryan, who picked up the metal case and carried into the house. He placed it on the central island in the kitchen.

"Is that the money?" asked Jonathan. He was standing in the doorway to the corridor wearing only a grey bath towel wrapped around his waist. His long dark hair hung around his shoulders.

"Perhaps you could put some clothes on," Sue requested.

Jonathan snorted, but turned and left the kitchen.

Malika's phone pinged.

"Ready?" asked Inspector Sue.

Malika nodded and tapped her phone. She then entered a code into the digital keypad on the case and they heard a clicking sound.

"Stand back," instructed Inspector Evans as he stepped forward, and taking the top of the case in both hands, he opened it.

Keya's first response was that the bank hadn't sent enough money, as the case wasn't full. But Ryan counted the bundles and checked them against the delivery note the inspector handed him, before nodding and confirming, "It's all here."

"Now what?" asked Jonathan, re-entering the kitchen. He was wearing black jogging pants and a grey t-shirt, and his hair was tied back in a bun.

"We wait," declared the inspector. "Sergeant Varma, put the kettle on. Time for a cuppa, I think." Inspector Evans turned his attention to Ryan. "And you better take up position by the entrance gate. I'll send the sergeant out with a cup of coffee for you."

"Yes, sir." Ryan placed his black police hat on his head and left the house.

Keya was just pouring hot water into mugs when Ryan charged back in, clasping his hat to his head. "Sir, you better see this," he blurted.

Inspector Evans looked serious as he followed Ryan outside. Malika and Jonathan both made to follow him, but Inspector Sue held her arm out and said, "Let them do their job."

"But he's our son," began Jonathan, and as he continued to argue with Inspector Sue, Keya sidestepped around them and rushed after Ryan and the Inspector.

She found them standing beside the front entrance gate post, staring at a red balloon.

"What's that?" she gasped breathlessly.

"What does it look like, Sergeant?" retorted the inspector in a sarcastic tone.

Keya answered, "A balloon, but do you think the person who left it was watching the house? And they waited for the ransom to be delivered and then, while we concentrated on the money, they left this?"

"Quite possibly," conceded the inspector.

"There's a note attached to the end of the ribbon," said Ryan as he squatted down. "And an empty black rucksack."

"That'll be for the money," muttered the inspector, as he pulled on a pair of blue latex gloves. "Untie the ballon and hand me the note."

Also wearing blue gloves, Ryan did as instructed and stood self-consciously holding the balloon as Inspector Evans tore open the white envelope. It was the same kind that had been delivered the previous day, but the inspector did not take the same care as the chief inspector had done in opening it.

Inspector Evans removed and unfolded a white sheet of A4 paper. "It's printed using a standard printer, I'd say," explained Inspector Evans.

"And what does it say?" Keya pressed.

"Put the money in the rucksack. Send the nanny to the 10.30 service at St. Mary's and tell her to sit on the end of the fifth row from the back, on the left side. Place the rucksack on the floor in the aisle at the end of the row. Don't send anyone else. No police. I will be watching. If you don't follow these instructions, you will never see the boy again. You have been warned."

CHAPTER FIFTEEN

Inspector Evans finished reading the ransom note and looked from Keya to Ryan, who was still holding the red balloon.

"Do you think she can do it?" asked the inspector.

"Who?" Keya asked.

"The nanny. Can she follow the instructions laid out in the letter?"

"To be honest, I've no idea. She's been blaming herself, so either she'll fall apart, or she'll see this as a way to make amends and help get Zaad back. I think you should speak to Inspector Sue and engage her help."

"Because she'll be able to sort the girl out?"

"Not exactly, but if anyone can prepare Biljana for the task, it's Inspector Sue."

"Very well," nodded the inspector. "And PC Jenkins, why are you standing there with that balloon? Pick up the rucksack."

Still clutching the balloon's gold ribbon, Ryan collected the rucksack and they all started to walk back to the house.

"What about proof of life, sir?" Keya asked.

"The chief inspector said there wasn't any contact with the child after he was taken yesterday."

"No, there wasn't. So we have no idea if he is still alive, or injured, or …."

"Don't say it, Sergeant," growled the inspector. "But this latest stunt doesn't help. And why the balloon?" Inspector Evans entered the house.

Keya followed Ryan and the balloon inside.

She heard Malika gasp.

"Are you OK?" Inspector Sue asked in a comforting tone.

"The balloon," whispered Malkia. "We bought one for Zaad at a fair last month. A red one, just like that. But he let go, and it flew away. He was so upset."

Keya turned away from Malika and muttered to Inspector Evans, "Does that count as proof of life?"

"Possibly. Although it's more likely someone close to the family is involved. Someone who knows about visits to the fair."

"Can I have the balloon?" Malika asked.

"It's evidence," snapped the inspector.

"Do you really think the kidnapper would leave his DNA?" countered Inspector Sue soothingly. "Surely it can't do any harm for Mrs Bartlett to have the balloon."

"If you say so," Inspector Evans conceded, grudgingly.

Ryan handed over the balloon and placed the rucksack on the counter. Then he lifted it up and shook it. "I think there's something inside."

Inspector Evans looked warily at the Bartletts. Malika stopped admiring the balloon and bit her lip as she stared at the rucksack. Jonathan tried to step forward, but Inspector Sue placed a restraining hand on his arm.

Ryan was still wearing his gloves, so Inspector Evans said, "Place the rucksack back on the counter and slowly and carefully unzip it. Stop the moment you see anything."

Ryan's face was flushed as he began unzipping the rucksack which he'd laid on the counter. It was the sort which unzipped all the way round and the front cover opened up, exposing the space inside.

Ryan stopped and looked up at Inspector Evans.

"Carry on."

Slowly and hesitantly, Ryan lifted the front of the rucksack to reveal … a book. A child's cardboard book entitled *Dear Zoo*.

Ryan laughed, probably in relief. "I remember this book. It has flaps inside which reveal where the different animals are hiding."

"Zaad loves it too," Jonathan announced, pushing past Sue and approaching the counter and rucksack. But that one looks new. Zaad's has a stain on the front where I spilt juice on it."

Inspector Evans murmured to Keya. "Still not proof of life. But more evidence to support my inside job theory."

Keya regarded the inspector. She was used to him thinking the worst of people, and having theories which were unpopular and made others uncomfortable. But she also knew, from experience, that his 'gut', as he called his intuition, was often right.

"So what do we do?"

"Continue with the plan. What other choice do we have? A young boy's life is at stake."

Inspector Evans cleared his throat. "Please don't touch the book. Constable, bag it as evidence. Now, accompanying these gifts left by the kidnapper was another letter ..."

"What does it say?" Jonathan demanded.

"It is a set of instructions. We've been told to place the ransom money in that rucksack and for Biljana to take it to church this morning. There are specific directions about where she should place it, which I'll discuss with her if you think she's up to the job, Sue."

"What exactly does she need to do?"

"Go to church. Sit in a designated spot and place the rucksack on the ground. That's all. The rest is up to us."

"Biljana usually attends church on a Sunday. Either here, or in Cirencester," said Malika, practically. "I think she'll find it comforting to go to today's service."

"If she already knows the church, it's layout, and some of the congregation, that will help. I'll go and speak to her." Inspector Sue left the kitchen.

"And I'll get dressed." Malika also left, followed by Jonathan.

Inspector Evans stretched his neck. "Perhaps now we can have that cup of coffee, and then you can take yours back to the entrance, Constable Jenkins, although I doubt we'll hear any more from our kidnapper."

Finally, only Keya and Inspector Evans were left in the kitchen.

Inspector Evans slurped his coffee while Keya gratefully sipped her tea.

"What we need," mused the inspector, "are eyes in the church. I'll speak to the vicar. Do you know him?"

"There's a new one in this parish, and I haven't met him yet. Aunt Beanie will know." Keya paused, and then exclaimed, "Aunt Beanie. She often goes to church. She could be our eyes and ears. And Norman, if we can persuade him to go too."

Inspector Evans scowled. "Isn't she likely to tackle the kidnapper head on if she sees him take the ransom money? We need someone dependable who will watch and wait, and inform us when the kidnapper makes his move."

"I'm sure we can persuade Aunt Beanie to do that. She does favour action, but if she knows she's to send a text message when she sees something, that might be enough."

"What about Inspector Sue?" suggested Inspector Evans. "She looks the church type."

"But won't the kidnapper have seen her, especially if, as you surmise, this is an inside job?"

"I think it's a risk I'm willing to take. There's no point handing over the money if we don't get the boy back."

Inspector Sue entered the kitchen and strode straight towards the kettle, which she switched on.

It soon boiled and while she made herself a coffee, she revealed, "Biljana is grateful to do something to help Zaad, and when I told her she would be going to church, she looked relieved."

"I'd like you to go too," Inspector Evans stated. "Not exactly with her, but to keep an eye on her and the bag."

"What if the kidnapper knows me?"

"That's why I suggested Aunt Beanie. She's a churchgoer and has nothing to do with the police."

"Good idea," agreed Sue. "She can sit near Biljana. I'm happy to go, but I think I should keep my distance and not spook the kidnapper."

"Very well," sighed Inspector Evans. He turned to Keya and said, "You better go and brief Aunt Beanie. And make sure she understands. No interfering."

Addressing Inspector Sue, he continued, "And if you're happy briefing Biljana, I'll go and speak to the vicar. But I'll be back in time to organise the ransom money."

CHAPTER SIXTEEN

When Keya returned to Meadowbank Farm, there were more signs of life than there had been earlier when she'd collected Ryan. Buttercup mooed from her pen in the barn, and the orange front door of the farmhouse stood open.

Keya admired the metal bucket of flowers she'd given Aunt Beanie, although she thought some new ones had been added. She smiled as she spotted the purple pansies before she entered the house.

The entrance porch, which Norman had decluttered, was returning to Aunt Beanie's state of living with a mismatch of items piled up against the wall, including a bright yellow watering can, a wicker basket, and a wooden chair propped at an angle as it only had three legs.

Keya made her way down the terracotta-tiled floor of the hallway to the kitchen at the far end of the house. She heard music playing, but when she opened the door, the kitchen was empty.

She was still standing in the doorway when she heard footsteps behind her, and she turned round to face Norman.

"Are you looking for Ryan? I thought you were picking him up early today."

"I was. I mean, I did. But I came back to speak to Aunt Beanie, and to you."

"Let me call Beanie. I know she's awake. I took a cup of tea up to her twenty minutes ago. Beanie," Norman called up a wooden staircase with a worn dark red floral carpet.

"Coming. What's the emergency?"

"Keya is here to see us."

"Is it the boy?" Aunt Beanie enquired, leaning over the first-floor balustrade.

"Yes, and we need your help."

"How exciting," cried the older woman as she descended the stairs. "Let's have breakfast, and you can tell us all about it."

Aunt Beanie and Keya sat at the kitchen table while Norman cooked breakfast. Keya told them about the balloon, the rucksack, the book, and finally the ransom letter.

As Norman placed a plate in front of her with two poached eggs on toast, accompanied by baked cherry tomatoes and slices of ripe green avocado, Keya concluded, "And that's where you come in."

"You want us to go to church this morning, undercover, don't you?" Aunt Beanie asked.

"We would like you to attend church, as neither Ryan, Inspector Evans, nor myself can go, but we only want you to watch. You have my number, so if you see anything, you text me. But you're not to make it obvious you're watching Biljana, or the rucksack of money."

Aunt Beanie clasped her hands together and exclaimed, "Oh, how exciting!"

"This is serious, Beanie," Norman chastised her as he sat down with his plate of eggs and bacon on toast. "A boy's life is at stake."

"I know," Aunt Beanie said, picking up her knife and fork, "But I miss my police work in the Art and Antiques Unit, and it feels good to be doing something useful again." The unit had been disbanded after the officer in charge had been forced to take early retirement.

"Do you need me?" asked Norman.

"I think it would help."

Norman nodded in understanding. His role was to supervise Aunt Beanie, as well as watch Biljana.

"And what about Monica and Marmaduke?"

"What about them?" asked Keya. She knew that Marmaduke Carey was Aunt Beanie's brother, but she had no idea who Monica was.

"They're joining us for Sunday lunch, now that Ryan is working."

Norman leaned towards Keya and explained, "Monica is Ryan's mum. His dad organised to meet up with friends, as Ryan was taking her to Kelmscott Manor, and we were all meeting up for lunch."

"So now Monica is coming here this morning, and I've invited Marmaduke to join us."

Keya hesitated. Aunt Beanie and Norman were one thing. They'd been involved in investigations before. In fact, Norman had once been questioned about killing a soldier. But Ryan's mum was a different matter.

"I'll talk to her when she arrives," suggested Aunt Beanie. "If she's not up for a bit of sleuthing, she can stay here while Norman and I attend church. Now, you do know it's a special service? The local children will be attending as they've prepared various crafts and flower arrangements which will be on display this morning."

"So the church will be full?"

"Not exactly, but there will be a larger congregation than usual," Aunt Beanie confirmed.

Keya didn't know if this was a good thing or not. An empty church would make Biljana and the rucksack more conspicuous, but a busy church meant it would be harder to watch them.

"The kidnapper's instructions are for Biljana to sit on the left of the church, in the fifth row from the back."

"Near the vestry entrance," Aunt Beanie observed.

"So where should you sit?"

"I normally sit near the front, but if I'm not too early ..."

"Which you won't be," Norman muttered.

Aunt Beanie ignored him. "The church will be busy and I can sit further back. Hopefully, behind the nanny."

Keya asked the obvious question. "Do you know what she looks like?"

"I know she's one of three young women looking after children in the town. And I'll know exactly which one from where she's sitting." Keya couldn't argue with that.

Aunt Beanie finished her breakfast, pushed her plate to one side, and said, "I better change for church."

"Now remember," Keya reminded her. "No heroics. You are only to observe and update me with messages."

Aunt Beanie's hand flew to her chest as she said, "As if I would do anything reckless."

Norman rolled his eyes.

CHAPTER SEVENTEEN

When Keya returned to the Bartletts' house on Cedar Drive, she found Inspector Evans apologising to Inspector Sue.

"And I'm afraid I didn't ask the vicar to help us," explained Inspector Evans.

"He's clearly anxious about conducting this morning's service, and telling him we are running a police operation in his church would only panic him."

"So I'm on my own," Inspector Sue concluded.

"Not exactly," said Keya as she approached the two inspectors. "You'll have the eyes and ears of Aunt Beanie and Norman."

She didn't mention Ryan's mum. After all, Monica was probably sensible and would choose to stay at Meadowbank Farm.

"Biljana's in the shower," Inspector Sue said, "so let's organise the ransom money." She entered the room off the kitchen and returned with Malika and the security briefcase.

Malika asked, "Is this the only way? How can we be sure the man who's sent us the notes is the kidnapper?"

"We can't," replied Inspector Evans. "But this is our only lead."

"What about the other ransom notes which arrived by email?"

Inspector Evans looked at Inspector Sue, who mouthed, "Copycat."

Keya hadn't known about any other ransom letters, and it appeared neither had the inspector, but his voice remained steadfast as he replied, "None of the people who sent those have contacted us again. This man is serious, and we have to treat his threats accordingly."

He looked round the kitchen.

Keya hoped he wasn't going to add, "And I doubt you'll miss the money."

Malika's arms hung limply by her sides as she said, "If you say so."

"All right. Can you open the security case again and I'll transfer the money into the rucksack?"

Malika stepped forward and entered the code. She stepped back as Inspector Evans opened the case and picked up the first wad of notes.

They all remained silent until the inspector had finished moving the money and zipped up the rucksack.

"Can I go too? To church," Malika pleaded.

"No, Mrs Bartlett. You and your husband will remain here with me. Inspector Sue will be in church, and Sergeant Varma will wait outside. The media team are lending their support and they'll be in their cars dotted around the town and covering all entrances to the church."

"But ..."

"Come on, Malika. Let's take you back to Jonathan." Inspector Sue escorted the still protesting Malika into the adjoining room.

"You'd better get going," Inspector Evans said to Keya as he handed her a radio from a group sitting on the central island.

"Only use this if you have to. Your phone will be less conspicuous but keep the radio on, as Inspector Unwin's team will provide regular updates. And find somewhere to sit outside the church, but nowhere obvious. Blend in."

Keya wasn't sure how an Indian woman, on her own, blended into an English country town on a Sunday morning, but she'd have to try.

"Yes, sir." Keya took the radio and, deciding to take her car, fished her car keys out of her jeans pocket.

She wound the window down as she braked to a stop beside Ryan, who was still on duty at the entrance gate.

"So this is it?" he said in a serious tone. "The family is paying the ransom, and you need to make sure they return the kid."

"Me, and the rest of the team," Keya replied, although, as she drove away, she did feel the burden of responsibility descend onto her shoulders.

She parked in the market square where, each Wednesday, stallholders still set up and sold a variety of goods from food to plants and crafts. She joined a steady flow of people walking towards the church, guided by the tolling of bells.

Aunt Beanie had been right. There were a lot of children accompanying their parents, well mainly their mothers, to the service today.

Keya entered the churchyard but stepped off the main path, walking towards the rear annex of the neighbouring town hall.

She found herself a shaded spot on the low wall and sat down, removing a pair of headphones and her phone from the cream tote bag she was carrying. Dotty had given it to her, and it had the image of a painting on it with a bridge over a pond of waterlilies.

Wearing the headphones and pretending to scroll through her phone, she hoped she looked like a single woman enjoying a quiet Sunday morning.

Five minutes later, a dark car stopped on the road and Biljana climbed out. Self-consciously, she walked through the entrance to the churchyard and along the gravel path. She kept patting her blonde hair and adjusting the rucksack which was hanging from her left shoulder.

Inspector Sue, wearing a huge pair of dark sunglasses, followed at a discrete distance.

Several minutes later, Keya spotted Aunt Beanie, who luckily did not see her. Norman looked unusually smart, and somewhat uncomfortable, in a grey suit. He was even wearing a tie.

They were unsuccessfully ignoring a short woman who was walking just behind them. Her grey hair was in a neat bob and she was dressed in a plain blue dress, but with the brightest yellow sandals. Was this Monica, Ryan's mum?

The bells stopped ringing, and a family rushed into the church. Then the churchyard was empty. Had the kidnapper entered the church before she arrived?

All she could do now was sit and wait.

CHAPTER EIGHTEEN

Even though Keya was wearing a pair of headphones to look as if she was concentrating on whatever she was listening to, they weren't sitting fully in her ears. Nor was she playing a podcast or any music through them.

From her cream tote bag, which sat beside her on the low boundary wall of the churchyard, she heard a crackle of static and a man's voice say, "All the congregation are now inside the church, over."

"Roger, out," said another voice, which sounded like her old colleague, Inspector Nick Unwin.

Her phone buzzed, and she glanced down at it.

Nanny and bag in place. Service started.

Keya heard the blended pipe sounds of the organ and then the voices of the congregation singing.

It was uplifting and very different from her less than frequent visits to her local Hindu temple, where those attending morning or evening worship did chant to music, but in a call and response fashion.

For her, religion was more about meditation and finding her inner self. She was drawn to the Hindu goddess Shakti, who represented the life force of the world, and the creation, maintenance, and destruction of the universe.

She was sometimes described as chaotic, which Keya identified with, but she was also about desire, knowledge, and, importantly, action. The power to act. And for Keya, this meant leading her own life and serving her community by seeking justice.

Her phone beeped with an incoming message.

Very busy here. The congregation are looking at the children's exhibits.

That did not sound good. Aunt Beanie, Norman and Sue might lose sight of Biljana, and more importantly, the bag.

Rucksack still in place.

Aunt Beanie texted. That was a relief.

As the service continued, Keya didn't receive any further updates until…

Final prayer

She stood up and, turning her back on the church, she leaned down towards her bag. Discretely picking up the radio, she pressed the talk button and said, "Service finishing. Bag still in place, over."

"Roger, out."

Keya returned to her position on the wall, but she was more alert and removed her headphones.

Anyone watching might think it strange anyway that she'd remained in one place for so long, and she doubted the kidnapper wouldn't have guessed she was a police officer.

The side door of the church opened, and several women and a vicar emerged carrying various bags and baskets.

They followed the path which led to a gate in the wall, further down from where Keya was sitting, and passed through it. As Keya watched them, one of the women looked up and smiled at her.

Keya maintained her distance at the end of the service as she watched the congregation leave by the main church door. Nobody was carrying the rucksack with the ransom money.

Her phoned pinged, and she looked down to read the message.

Come Quick

Grabbing her bag, Keya jumped off the wall and ran across the graveyard, dodging headstones, until she reached the front door.

Another vicar was thanking the departing congregation for attending and inviting them to the town hall for refreshments. He watched her wide-eyed as she pushed through the exiting crowd and entered the church.

Part way down the left aisle, Aunt Beanie was hugging Biljana, and as Keya approached, she heard the nanny's loud sobs. Beyond them, Norman held up the rucksack for Inspector Sue to look inside.

This did not look good.

Aunt Beanie smiled sadly as Keya passed her and approached Norman and Inspector Sue.

"He's tricked us," Inspector Sue stated flatly. "Taken the money and left the bag."

"Or switched the one with money for this empty one," Norman suggested.

Keya gasped. "Of course. He gave us the rucksack. It makes sense he had a duplicate one, as it would be easier to switch them rather than pick up our one and walk away with it."

"And the area next to Biljana was very busy when members of the congregation were invited to look at the children's exhibits on these tables." Inspector Sue indicated to two tables pushed against the outside wall.

Keya stepped closer and looked down at a series of flower arrangements in unusual objects, including a teacup and saucer, a child's red wellington boot, and three eggshells in a cardboard egg box.

She looked up at Inspector Sue and said, "But I didn't see anyone leave with a rucksack."

"Perhaps it's still here, and he intends to return for it later," Norman responded, glancing around the church.

"But what about Zaad? Where is he?" asked Inspector Sue.

"Did the kidnapper leave a note for Biljana?"

"No." Inspector Sue's brow wrinkled, and she looked at Keya with a pained expression.

"Let's search the church before we jump to conclusions," Keya suggested.

"But we're running out of time," Inspector Sue lamented.

Keya was used to the calm, collected version of the police inspector.

She lowered her voice and said, "We don't know that. This might all be part of the plan. The kidnapper knows we're involved. That's why he sent someone else with the note yesterday, and waited until we were distracted with the money before leaving this morning's message. I'll call Nick and see if his team can help search the church."

"What's happening?" Nick asked, immediately answering his phone.

"We've lost the money, and we've not heard from the kidnapper. Can you send some of your team to help search the church in case the boy, a note, or the ransom money is here?"

"I'll be with you in a few minutes."

As Keya finished the call, she looked towards the church entrance, where she saw the vicar glance inside before disappearing again. Clearly, he didn't want to be involved.

"There, there," Aunt Beanie consoled Biljana. "It wasn't your fault. We were here with you, and we didn't notice anything."

"But poor Zaad," sobbed Biljana, pulling herself out of Aunt Beanie's embrace.

"I'm sure he'll be fine. Look, here are more police officers to help find him."

Nick, wearing a smart, and probably expensive, charcoal grey suit, directed members of his team to search areas of the church.

Keya wandered across to another door, located beside the table of flower arrangements, and tried the large metal handle. The door opened smoothly, and she entered the church vestry.

Along one wall there was a large wooden wardrobe with high-level cupboards. There was a metal rail in front of it holding the vicar's white vestments and black and purple stoles.

On the far wall, there was a mirror above a sink, with a low cupboard on one side and a set of shelves, with neatly arranged files and papers, on the other. Next to another door, there was a small desk.

Keya crossed to the door and tried the handle. It opened, and she walked out into the graveyard, looking down the path towards a small gate in the wall which she'd been sitting on earlier.

The only people who'd left that way had been the women who she presumed were preparing the after-service refreshments.

She returned to the main section of the church where a despondent group of Inspector Sue, Biljana, and Aunt Beanie, who still had an arm around the upset nanny, were watching Norman and Nick's team search the church.

"What's in there?" Nick asked, pointing to the door Keya had just walked through.

"The vestry."

Nick indicated to a man, and they both entered the adjacent room.

"Have you spoken to Inspector Evans?" Keya asked Inspector Sue.

"No, I wanted to wait until after the search and …" her voice trailed off.

"You'd prefer it if I called him?"

Inspector Sue gave her a lopsided smile. "I'm better at dealing with families than senior police officers."

Keya walked through the church and called Inspector Evans as she stepped out of the main door.

"Update," said the inspector, answering her call.

Keya told him.

"Not good, but not exactly a surprise. Inside job, mark my words," said the inspector.

"But it doesn't help us locate Zaad."

"True. Continue your search and keep me informed. And send Sue back with the nanny. I'll need her to break the news to the parents."

As Keya finished the call, the vicar who'd been saying goodbye to the departing congregation approached her and said, "I presume you're the police. An inspector came to see me this morning, but he didn't really say what he wanted. I don't like to interfere, but is there anything I can help you with?"

"Did you hear about the missing boy?"

"Do you think he's in the church?"

"Not exactly. It's not common knowledge, but the family received a ransom demand and instructions for their nanny to bring the money here."

"To church?" The vicar's voice rose in pitch.

"Yes. And Biljana's very upset as the money is now missing, along with the boy."

"That's terrible. Let me speak to Biljana. I've got to know her and her compatriots since I joined the parish. Nice girls."

As the vicar moved away, Keya called to him, "And what about the other vicar? Is he still serving refreshments in the town hall?"

"Other vicar? No, I'm the only one in this parish."

CHAPTER NINETEEN

Keya ran out of the front of the church and down the path to the boundary wall.

Hastily pulling open the gate, she rushed through, crying "Ow!" as she caught her leg on the protruding latch.

She stopped briefly to rub her leg, before continuing at a swift walk towards the back door of the church hall extension. Passing the coloured wheelie bins she froze, before moving across to the black one.

A piece of white material was caught in the lid and, lifting it up, she pulled out a white tunic, like the one the vicar had been wearing.

That both vicars had worn. Holding it up, she realised that the man she'd presumed was a vicar, when he left through the church's side door, must have grabbed it from the rail in the vestry.

She peered back into the bin and something black and hairy caught her eye. Reaching in, she removed a wig.

She couldn't picture the vicar who'd been with the women leaving the church service early, but it was likely he'd worn the wig and then discarded it. Not having an evidence bag large enough for the wig and tunic, she carried them back to the church.

It was quiet inside.

Inspector Sue approached her, staring at the things she was

carrying and said, "Nick and his team have returned to Cedar Lane. They didn't find anything, but it looks as if you did?"

"The disguise our kidnapper used to get away. To evade us. And he walked right past me," Keya said dejectedly.

"When?" asked Inspector Sue.

"Just before the end of the service. With a group of ladies who I presumed were leaving early to prepare refreshments. And they were all carrying bags."

"Any rucksacks?"

"No, but it would be easy enough to hide the rucksack inside a basket, or another bag."

"I need to take Biljana back. What are you going to do?"

"Speak to the ladies I saw earlier. See if any of them knew or spoke to the pretend vicar."

Inspector Sue and Keya walked down the aisle to Biljana, Aunt Beanie and Norman, who were with the real vicar.

"I really am sorry, and if there is anything I can do to help, or if you'd like me to come to the house, Biljana, please call me."

Biljana nodded.

"Thank you, vicar," said Aunt Beanie before turning to the two policewomen. "And we better rescue Monica from serving teas and coffees."

"Ryan's mum? Did she leave the service early?" Keya asked.

"Yes," confirmed Aunt Beanie. "Deidre asked me to help, as there were so many people in the congregation this morning, but, of course, I couldn't leave my post, so Monica volunteered."

"I need to speak to her."

"Lovely. I know she'd like to meet you."

Keya turned to leave, and Aunt Beanie called, "Aren't you going to leave the vicar's vestments here?"

"No, they're evidence." Keya pushed the white tunic and black wig into her tote bag, which bulged with the additional items.

As Keya, Norman, and Aunt Beanie walked along the main church path, onto the pavement and through the front door of the adjoining three-storey stone town hall, Keya explained how the kidnapper had evaded all of them.

"Monica will be so excited to be involved," enthused Aunt Beanie.

"Beanie," growled Norman.

"Of course," said Aunt Beanie, contritely. "I'm sure she'll be eager to help your investigation."

They entered a crowded room and Aunt Beanie raised her hand as if signalling to someone. The crowd parted as Aunt Beanie pushed through to the back and Keya and Norman followed her.

"Tea," said Aunt Beanie, pushing a cup and saucer into Keya's hand. "And this is Monica." To the woman with a neat grey bob and short fringe, Aunt Beanie said, 'Monica, you've done a sterling job. Why don't you take a break and join Keya outside?"

Keya carried her tea out of the room, but cried, "Ow," when someone's knee knocked into her leg in the same place as she'd caught it on the gate latch.

"Are you OK?" asked Monica as they stepped outside and onto the pavement.

"Yes," Keya replied through gritted teeth. "I've hurt my leg, that's all."

"Would you like me to look at it? I was a nurse."

Keya could imagine Ryan's mum caring for other people and comforting them. She had the same round, open and honest face as her son, although she was much smaller than him.

"I think I'll be all right, but thanks." Keya shifted her tote bag on her shoulder. "I wanted to ask you about the priest who accompanied you to the church hall during today's service."

Monica frowned. "Strange man for a vicar. A bit … working-class for the role, not that I'm saying vicars can't be working class. But he didn't speak like a man of the people. Rather, he grunted. And to be honest, I haven't seen him since we started preparing the after-service refreshments."

"What did he look like?" Keya asked.

"Well like a vicar, with a white robe, although he didn't have a black cassock underneath, he was wearing dark trousers and a pair of sturdy black boots."

Monica glanced down at her bright yellow sandals. Then she continued, "And he was thickset, but not overweight, and clean shaven, but with a stippling of stubble."

"And when did he join you?"

"He was already in the vestry when we entered, adjusting his black hair in the mirror. His hair was a bit strange, straggly and rather untidy for a man of the cloth."

"Like this?" asked Keya, removing the wig from her bag.

Monica gasped. "Of course, he was wearing a wig. That explains it. But why?"

"To disguise himself. So he joined your party as you left the vestry?"

"Yes. He picked up a black bag with one of those sporting brand logos on the side and joined us as we walked across to the back of the town hall. And as I said, I didn't see him again after we came into the hall and turned on the urns for the hot water."

Keya looked up and down the street.

"Did I do something wrong?" asked Monica in a concerned voice.

"No, you didn't do anything wrong," Keya replied. "But I did. This is my fault."

CHAPTER TWENTY

"It is not your fault," declared Inspector Evans in the kitchen of the Bartletts' home in Cedar Drive.

Keya stood facing him, her arms hanging limply by her sides.

"How were you to know that wasn't the new vicar, or a curate? It's Inspector Onion I'll be having words with, and asking why his team didn't spot a lone man carrying a large sports bag away from the church."

Keya took a deep breath and said, "To be fair, sir, they were all in their cars and the man could have taken the path which runs alongside the river and under the bridge. He could have parked his car in one of a number of streets on the southern side of Fairford."

"So where does this leave us?" Inspector Evans asked.

Keya rather felt that was a question she should be asking her boss. She replied dully, "Without the money or the boy."

"Exactly. Now we might be lucky. If this man was the kidnapper, he might send us another note with the location of the boy. Or, knowing the family will pay up, he may demand more money, or …"

"Or what, sir?"

"He had nothing to do with it in the first place, and we're back to square one and the family is £48,000 worse off."

Inspector Evans and Keya were silent, and Keya considered the possibilities Inspector Evans had laid out. Had they really spent all their time and energy focusing on someone who had nothing to do with Zaad's disappearance?

Or perhaps he was the kidnapper, and had no intention of returning Zaad, or maybe - she hated to think about it - the poor boy was dead.

Ryan entered the kitchen and halted, looking from Keya to Inspector Evans and back to Keya. "Mum said you lost the kidnapper."

"Constable Jenkins, how does your mother know about this case? We haven't given that information to the public."

"Actually, sir," Keya answered, "Monica, Ryan's mum, was part of the team in the church today. And she actually spoke to the man we believe took the money as she and some other ladies left the service."

Ryan crossed the kitchen and turned on the kettle. "She feels very stupid that she didn't spot he was wearing a wig. She only really noticed his white vicar's robe. Although she did wonder what he was carrying in his sports bag."

"£48,000, that's what," declared the inspector. He turned and strode across the room to the kitchen's patio windows, stopped, and looked outside, and then turned and strode back.

Ryan made tea for himself and Keya, and a coffee for the inspector, as Inspector Evans continued to pace up and down the kitchen.

Eventually, the inspector stopped and said, "We need to progress this case in two directions. Firstly, we assume the boy will be returned today and all we need to do is be patient. But we also need to accept that we may have been focusing on the wrong party, and that the kidnapper and the boy are still out there. As Mrs Bartlett reminded us, there were several other ransom notes which the team dismissed as copycats yesterday. But perhaps one of them was genuine."

The inspector crossed to the central island and picked up his mug of coffee. "I'll ask for some other officers to come over and cover for you two, as I want you to go somewhere quiet and work through all the correspondence the Bartletts have received from Friday through to today."

"What are we looking for?" asked Ryan.

"Anything which you think looks genuine," replied the inspector. "Little details about the child, which we can check with the family, or his abduction. I'm sure that the chief inspector was right to dismiss most of those other demands, but perhaps hidden amongst them is correspondence from the real kidnapper."

Ryan frowned, and asked, "So why didn't he contact us again?"

"Maybe he, or she, will, Constable, now that we are no longer concentrating on balloon man, as I'm going to refer to him. The real kidnapper might not have wanted his message lost amongst that of the balloon man's, and now he has the stage again. But I really don't know."

Inspector Sue opened the door from the room Keya now knew was the snug, where the Bartletts were.

"Jonathan is very angry," she declared. "With us. With the kidnapper. With the world. And I've put Malika to bed. It was all too much for her."

"And Biljana?" asked Keya.

"She's really upset and blaming herself. She can't believe that the rucksack was switched while she was watching it, but then she is a devout Christian and I'm sure her automatic reaction was to close her eyes while praying, or concentrate on the vicar, rather than those around her."

Keya added, "Aunt Beanie sent me a message to say it was a bit chaotic when the congregation was invited to look at the children's exhibits at the tables near where Biljana was sitting. I expect that's when the bags were swapped."

"I need access to the Bartletts' email accounts," Ryan mused, "and any other places where they received messages."

"Inspector Unwin's team has all of that. Why don't you go through to the living room and speak with them?"

Picking up his tea, Ryan disappeared into the room behind the kitchen, which Chief Inspector Greg had vacated to allow the media team to use it.

"Now what?" asked Inspector Sue.

"What do you usually do in such cases?" countered Inspector Evans.

Inspector Sue glanced down at the grey-tiled floor. With a pained expression, she looked up and replied, "Prepare for the worst. If a kidnap victim is not returned within the first forty-eight hours of being abducted, they rarely turn up alive."

"So we still have time," Keya concluded.

"Some, but no leads to pursue, unless I'm wrong?" Inspector Sue looked across at Inspector Evans.

"You're not. I think we all need a break and to come at this with fresh eyes. Sue, you should go home and see your family, and I'm sending Sergeant Varma and Constable Ryan away to look at other leads. Distance might give you all perspective."

"What about you, sir? What were you supposed to be doing today?" asked Keya.

"Going to my mother's for lunch, as I always do on a Sunday, except when I'm working. But she's used to it. I told her yesterday that I was unlikely to be there, but I'll give her a call."

Keya had met the inspector's mother, and she was a formidable woman, although, from the few bits of information the inspector had let slip, while her mind was still razor sharp, her body was starting to fail her.

Ryan reappeared carrying a laptop, and the inspector said, "Off you go, all of you. I'll stay here with the family."

CHAPTER TWENTY-ONE

"I'll drop you back home," Keya said as she and Ryan climbed into her VW Polo. She drove the short distance back to Meadowbank Farm, only subliminally aware of the pleasant summer weather.

A young boy was out there, and at the moment, she had no way of finding him.

As they crossed over the River Coln, she did notice the cows grazing contentedly in the meadow, and as they turned into Meadowbank Farm, her phone buzzed.

She parked in front of the gate leading to the farmhouse's orange door before answering the call.

"Hi, Sis," she said, seeing her sister's name on the screen.

"Is everything all right? Amma said you're not at the cafe as you've been called away on police business."

"That's right. And I should check she's OK. But, at the moment, my priority is finding a missing boy."

"The toddler from Fairford?"

"Yes, how do you know about that?"

"It was on Corinium Radio, a local community station Maitri found for us this morning."

"Maitri? What's she doing with you?"

"One of Aadi's, sorry, our neighbours, has recently separated from her husband and has had to go back to work. She needs someone to look after her kids for the shifts her mum and friends can't do. So Maitri volunteered.

"It's good for her to earn some money and have some responsibility. The girls she's looking after are young enough to still enjoy dolls and crafts. Maitri came back with a bead bracelet they'd made for her yesterday evening."

"That's great, and perhaps she'll start thinking seriously about her future."

"She's young, Keya. Leave her be. But are you OK?"

"Yes, just worried about the missing boy."

"Well, Aadi's back to work tomorrow, so don't worry about the cafe. I'll be in on Tuesday. Just find the poor child."

Keya thought she heard Aadi's voice in the background.

"Better go," said Zivah. "We're all going to puja at the temple near Aadi's parents, and then back to theirs for lunch. I think Appa is joining us."

"Thanks for calling."

Ryan had removed himself from Keya's car while she was speaking to Zivah, but he now reappeared, walking down the path from the farmhouse.

Keya opened her car door.

"Aunt Beanie insists you stay for lunch, although it won't be for a couple of hours. That gives us time to work through the case together while we're waiting."

Keya contemplated returning to her little house, but the prospect wasn't appealing. She needed to be with people at the moment, and working on the case with Ryan was much better than looking at it on her own. She climbed out of her car.

Seated at the long pine table in the kitchen at Meadowbank Farm, with a cup of tea in front of her, Keya opened the laptop Ryan had brought with him.

Ryan, who had changed and was now wearing a pair of jeans and pink polo shirt instead of his police uniform, was using his own police-issue laptop, but his personal one was also on the table, its lid closed.

"I'm sorry we couldn't visit Kelmscott Manor today," Ryan said to his mum, who was peeling potatoes.

"Don't worry, love. Besides, it was fun being part of the police operation today. I've never understood why you joined the police force, when you had so many better paid opportunities with computers, but I think I understand now. Your work is far more hands on, and you deal with real issues."

"Something like that," muttered Ryan, shifting uncomfortably on his wooden chair.

Aunt Beanie entered the kitchen and announced, "That's Agatha's sty cleaned out. How are you getting on in here, Monica?"

"The chickens are in the oven, and I've peeled the potatoes and carrots, and sliced the beans."

"Marvellous. Do you fancy half an hour helping me in the garden? You can deadhead while I weed."

"Sure," replied Monica and she followed Aunt Beanie out of the kitchen.

Relieved to have the kitchen to themselves, Keya said, "Let's start at the beginning. The case file says that Biljana called the police at 11.40 on Saturday morning from The Walnut Tree Playing Field, Fairford."

"Correct," agreed Ryan, reading through the information on his screen.

"Two officers were dispatched and arrived at the fenced play park area just after midday. They met a tearful Biljana, who insisted she'd looked everywhere and couldn't find Zaad. Both officers helped search the area and then one officer stayed at The Walnut Tree Playing Field while the other escorted Biljana back to Cedar Lane."

Keya clicked on another file. "The officer who remained collected a number of witness statements. Let's read through them and see if anything jumps out."

Keya sipped her tea as she read.

"I can't believe how little people actually see," Ryan commented.

"I know, but most don't live in the moment. They're distracted by other things, usually their phones."

"Not one person remembers seeing a little boy."

Keya sat back. "They probably would if he'd been upset and crying out."

"So you think he went willingly, because he knew his abductor?"

"Or he was tempted by something. Like an ice cream." Keya continued, "Chief Inspector Greg's two hypotheses at the start were that either Zaad had wandered off by himself, or someone had abducted him."

"But," Ryan added, "he dismissed the first hypothesis after police and locals searched the area, and the ransom note was received at the house."

"A ransom note which might not have come from the abductor. Perhaps from someone who was at The Walnut Tree Playing Field and saw the commotion?" suggested Keya.

"They'd need to be quick thinking, to go home to write and print out the note before delivering it to Cedar Drive."

"So they also knew where the family lived. What time was the note delivered?" Keya asked.

"13.20. Just after the police officer escorted Biljana back to the house."

"That would give the balloon man time to prepare the note, if he'd seen what was happening at the playing fields and lived locally. But what about anyone else?"

"I've seen photos and videos from The Walnut Tree Playing Field yesterday morning and a lot more people were there than gave witness statements. But it'll take a while tracking them all down."

"Time we don't have," Keya remarked. She leaned forward and started reading the case notes again.

"So Jonathan was already at home when Biljana arrived with her police escort, and his immediate reaction was anger vented against Biljana for losing Zaad."

"A natural reaction," suggested Ryan.

"Yes," agreed Keya, "But not a helpful one. Where had he been all morning?"

They both clicked keys on their respective laptops.

"It doesn't say."

Keya picked up her phone and called Inspector Evans.

"Yes, Sergeant?"

"Ryan, Constable Jenkins and I are working through the case notes, but it doesn't say where Mr Bartlett was on Saturday morning. Can you ask him?'

"Hold on."

Keya heard a clunk, perhaps as the phone was put down, and the sound of a door opening and then voices.

She clicked on her laptop, returning to the witness statements, and then she heard a woman's angry voice from her phone shout, "You said you were going to talk to a man about your paintings."

Keya didn't hear the reply.

"You're a liar, and a cheat, and it's time you stood on your own two feet." It sounded like a door slammed.

Inspector Evans' voice said, "That was illuminating. It appears Mr Barlett told his wife he was going to see a man about his paintings. But what he actually did was go to a private viewing for a new exhibition of local artists. One being run by some friends of yours."

"Jarrod Willcox?" Keya had met him during an earlier case, and he'd been very helpful in distinguishing original artwork from forgeries.

"Yes, him, and the young artist, Finn Andrews, and Lady Violet Stanley-Rudd."

Keya had met them all through her police work and Aunt Beanie had even been part of their team for a short time.

To the inspector she said, "Malika sounded very upset."

"Yes, Mrs Bartlett is upset. She thought her husband was actually trying to sell his work, rather than rub noses with the great and good of Cotswold society."

Ryan had opened his personal laptop, and turned the screen towards Keya, who looked at the heading, "Successful Exhibition Opening" and then the photographs of various well-dressed people.

Ryan pointed to a photo. It was a picture of Jonathan standing with three attractive, smiling women.

CHAPTER TWENTY-TWO

Keya finished her call to Inspector Evans.

Sitting next to her at the wooden table in the kitchen at Meadowbank Farm, Ryan reasoned, "No wonder Jonathan was angry when Biljana returned without Zaad. He was covering his own guilt for spending the morning at the art exhibition rather than being with his son."

"Hmm," Keya muttered.

"What?"

"How do you think his wife felt? She was at work, so unable to spend Saturday morning with her boy. But her husband chooses to spend time with the local yummy mummies rather than with Zaad. And Malika's the one actually paying the nanny to look after their son."

Silence fell between them.

"OK, let's get back to the case," Keya suggested. "We've got as far as Biljana and her police escort arriving home and telling Jonathan that Zaad was missing. What happened next? Was it the ransom note?"

"Yes, that arrived at 13.20. And I didn't know this. The letter was thrown into the drive and the police officer who'd escorted Biljana home thought it was thrown by a boy on a bicycle, but he couldn't be certain because the bike rider was wearing a cycle helmet."

"But if we find the bike rider, we'll have a witness who might be able to describe the balloon man."

"Or it could have been the balloon man."

"OK. That may be something to pursue, but let's park it for the moment," Keya decided. "What were the other ransom notes, and how were they delivered?"

"One person called Radio Cirencester, and the radio station also received an email, as did another station I've never heard of called Corinium Radio ..."

"That's the local station Zivah told me about earlier."

"Is it? I'll have to check it out. Do you want to hear the recording from Radio Cirencester?" Ryan asked.

"Yes. Good idea."

Ryan pressed a key on his police laptop.

Keya and Ryan listened as a man said, "I have the boy. If you want to see him again, stop the closure of Stratton village allotments, and the building of the new executive housing estate. Otherwise it will be more than marrows you'll be digging up."

"I hope he's not for real," Keya remarked. "But he sounds like a local activist rather than a kidnapper. And he has a point. The local residents don't want more large houses being built, especially if it destroys their allotments. Many of them grow flowers and vegetables on their small pieces of land, or just use them as somewhere to meet up with friends."

She sighed and then asked, "What about the emails?"

"This one is very polite, and apologises but says they desperately need money, so if the Bartletts leave £10,000 in an envelope at the front desk of the radio station, God will bless them and return their son."

"Sounds like a chancer, don't you think?"

"You mean that the person who wrote the email doesn't actually have the boy?"

"Exactly. And the one sent to Corinium Radio?" asked Keya.

"It says that if the family wants to see their child again, they must pay £25,000, of which £5,000 must be in £10 notes, £10,000 in £20 notes and £10,000 in £50 notes. Then the money must be put in a Waitrose shopping bag, and left in the dustbin by the trolley shelter in row K of the car park at the Cirencester branch of Waitrose, between eleven o'clock and eleven-fifteen on Monday morning."

"What?" exclaimed Keya.

"I know. Another hoax?"

"Sounds like it. But if we have nothing to do tomorrow morning, we could always sit and wait for them in the Waitrose car park. So those are all dead ends?"

"It looks like it," Ryan agreed. "But there were several messages sent to the family's email address."

Feeling despondent, Keya replied, "Let's hear them."

Ryan clicked on one and read, "The good Lord has punished your heathen ways ..."

"Enough," cried Keya. "Next."

"We have Zaad. If you want to see him again, you must follow our instructions. Do NOT contact the police. The amount for his safe return is £250,000 wired to a Rebellion account. Set up and verify your account. Wait for further instructions on the transfer."

Keya sat up. This one sounded authentic. Simple. To the point. And an amount worth the trouble of taking a small boy. Although she wasn't sure what a Rebellion account was.

Ryan stared at the email and then said, "That makes sense. Rebellion is a multi-currency exchange site which has no transfer limits."

"But banks do, even for electronic money, don't they?" Keya queried.

"Yes, although it depends on the client. It's actually difficult to transfer such a large amount in one go. You can't just make a PayPal transaction."

"So whoever sent that email had thought the process through. And the amount of money demanded is more in keeping with a family who've recently bought an expensive new house, and who have a high disposable income. Are you sure the person who sent this didn't send a follow-up email?"

Ryan tapped his keyboard, and Keya waited.

"No, nothing from the same email address, which, by the way, was probably made up just to send that email."

"Why do you say that?"

"Because the address is DontTraceMe@gmail.com."

"And can you trace them? Or is it just a taunt?"

Aunt Beanie and Monica entered the kitchen.

"Any progress?" asked Aunt Beanie, cheerfully. She was carrying a bunch of flowers which included pink roses.

"Not really," replied Keya flatly.

Ryan ignored them and continued tapping keys until he announced, "I've found them. The email was sent from an IP address in central Cirencester. Probably from a restaurant. Or other public Wi-Fi system."

"Can you be more specific?" asked Keya.

"I can try."

Aunt Beanie opened the top door of the Aga oven, and the aroma of roast chicken filled the kitchen.

Ryan sniffed, momentarily distracted, before returning to his work. "Here we are. The Copper Kettle."

"That's in a courtyard, behind the TSB Bank, off Market Place." Keya pushed back her chair with renewed enthusiasm. "Let's go!"

"What? It's lunchtime and I'm starving."

Keya gave Ryan a sympathetic look and replied, "Remember, a young boy's life is at stake."

CHAPTER TWENTY-THREE

Keya drove a reluctant Ryan into Cirencester.

As it was Sunday afternoon, the town was quiet. She easily found a parking space in the designated area in the centre of the wide Market Street.

People were still wandering about in t-shirts and shorts but, after the warm sunny weather they'd been enjoying, there was a chill in the air. Small gusts of winds were picking up and then dropping the flags hanging limply from the flagpoles protruding from The Fleece pub.

Looking up, Keya noticed clouds gathering in the azure blue sky.

The bank was closed, and Ryan ducked under a stone arch as they entered a narrow alleyway running alongside it.

Several groups of customers occupied metal tables and chairs outside a single-storey stone building, which had probably once been a store or workshop.

A tired-looking waitress stopped clearing plates from a table and said, "We close in half an hour, but I can get you something to drink and perhaps a slice of cake?"

Ryan looked hopeful, but Keya removed her warrant card and, opening it discreetly said, "Another time. We're here on official business."

The waitress' eyes widened.

"We're looking for someone who was here yesterday lunchtime and sent an email using your internet."

"We were busy yesterday, and most of our customers had phones. Toby was here, as usual, and he works on a tablet. Does that help?"

"Do you know Toby's full name, or where he lives?" asked Keya.

"Let me ask inside." The waitress placed the remaining plates on her tray, picked it up, and carried it into the cafe building.

Keya looked around. "There are no CCTV cameras here, although the bank's likely to have one on the front of their building, and at the rear."

"Our emailer could have been anyone." Ryan looked despondent as he lowered his chin to his chest.

Keya thought he was probably frustrated to be on a seemingly hopeless work visit instead of tucking into a roast Sunday lunch with his mum.

"They wouldn't even need to be here to send it," he added.

"Why not?" asked Keya sharply.

"They could have scheduled it. But then …" Ryan stopped and looked around. "They would have needed to leave their device."

"You mean they could have written the email and then dumped the phone?"

"Yes. Exactly."

"We'll ask the waitress if anyone has left an electronic device, but let's have a look around while we wait."

There wasn't much to search. The tables and metal chairs were in a flagstone yard. At one end there was an old stone trough, filled with red and white geraniums. Keya checked it for a mobile phone, but nobody had placed one amongst the flowers.

"Here," called Ryan.

Keya turned and saw him place a blue-gloved hand into a fluted topped metal and wood slatted dustbin.

As she approached him, he pulled out a black mobile phone.

"What are you doing?" asked the waitress in an irritated voice as she joined them.

"How often is this bin emptied?" Keya countered.

"The council does it every Thursday. Why?"

"Did you see anyone place this in here?"

"No. Do you think they did it by mistake? Nobody reported a missing phone."

"And you didn't find another one at the cafe yesterday, did you?"

"No," the waitress replied suspiciously.

"Is your Wi-Fi password protected?" Ryan asked.

The waitress crossed her arms. "Just what is this all about?" she demanded.

"It's part of an ongoing investigation," Keya informed her. "Please answer my colleague's question."

"Yes," she replied huffily. "And it's only for customers."

"And do you change the password regularly?"

"I've no idea. It's nothing to do with me."

Keya said, "When customers ask for the Wi-Fi code, where do they find it?"

"I tell them, or it's written on the blackboard inside."

"And what is it?"

"This month it's Avocado with a capital A."

"Thank you," said Keya, making sure she sounded grateful.

The waitress unfolded her arms and held out a piece of paper. "This is Toby's full name, from yesterday's receipt. And one of the cooks thinks he lives in Stratton."

"Thank you," Keya repeated. "You've been very helpful. And can I just check? Do you have any security cameras?"

"No. The owner thought it was safer to only take card payments. There's no cash on the premises."

"As I thought," Keya said as she and Ryan walked back up the alleyway and into Market Street.

"What now?" asked Ryan.

"Back to Meadowbank Farm for lunch."

Ryan smiled as he folded himself into Keya's little blue car.

CHAPTER TWENTY-FOUR

When Keya and Ryan arrived back at Meadowbank Farm, Aunt Beanie was serving coffee to Norman and Monica.

Aunt Beanie removed a bottle of red wine from in front of her brother, Marmaduke Carey, who was also Gilly Wimsey's father, and said, "And that's quite enough of that if you're driving. Coffee?"

"Black," replied Marmaduke, eyeing the retreating bottle.

"Oh good. You're back," said a relieved Monica as Ryan approached the kitchen table. "Do you both have time for lunch, or do you have to rush off again?"

"I'm not going anywhere until I've eaten," said Ryan, looking around the empty table.

"That's my boy." Monica smiled proudly at him as she pushed back her chair and rose to her feet.

"We put your lunch on a plate and kept it warm in the bottom oven of the Aga." Monica turned to Keya, and said, "And Beanie made you a small pasta dish with spinach, artichokes and parmesan cheese."

"Wonderful," said Keya gratefully, as she washed her hands in the sink under a small window, and admired a jam jar arrangement of wildflowers.

"Do you mind if we catch the afternoon news?" asked Marmaduke, and without waiting for a reply, he picked up the remote control from a bookshelf and switched on a small TV which sat on top of it.

As Keya carried her plate of pasta, to which she'd added edible-pod peas and green beans - 'from the garden' Aunt Beanie had told her - she immediately recognised the entrance to the Bartletts' house on the television screen.

A crowd of reporters were gathered outside it, and a young constable, whom Keya recognised from Cirencester station, looked anxious as he tried to stop them pushing forward between the gateposts.

The camera panned across to show a stylish-looking Inspector Nick Unwin, wearing his charcoal grey suit, unhurriedly leave the house and approach the reporters.

He stopped in front of them and said, "Please, step back out of the driveway. I will provide you with a full update, but you need to observe the family's privacy, and their boundaries."

Nobody appeared to move, so Nick stood silently and coolly while the camera continued to focus on him. Eventually, it moved back.

Nick took a step forward and began, "I'm very sorry to announce the disappearance of two-year-old Zaad Bartlett."

As Nick explained about the boy's disappearance, a dishevelled looking Inspector Evans stepped out of the house and glumly surveyed the reporters.

"He speaks very well, doesn't he," said Aunt Beanie from the end of the table as she sipped her coffee and watched Nick.

"Better than that Welshman lurking by the front door," muttered Marmaduke.

"How is the inspector's mother?" asked Aunt Beanie. "I must go and visit her. We've missed her at the horticultural society this year. I think she'd enjoy our planned visit to Kiftsgate Court Gardens next month. Perhaps I should offer to drive her."

"She's OK," Ryan replied, "although I think the inspector is worried about her. She's had several falls, but none of them have been serious."

"So far," mused Aunt Beanie. "She's tough, but there comes a time when we all need help."

Norman, who'd been watching the TV, turned and asked, "So the boy wasn't returned this morning, after the ransom money was paid?"

"No," Keya replied glumly, "probably because the person who took it had nothing to do with his actual abduction."

"Is that why the press are now involved? To try to find him?" Norman queried.

"Possibly, although Nick did well to keep them at bay this long. A missing toddler and a ransom note is quite a story."

On screen, Keya heard Nick say, "The family's only concern is their son, which is why they have offered a £200,000 reward for his safe return."

Keya choked on her pasta. After sipping from a glass of water, she remarked, "Wow. That's new."

"The reward?" asked Monica.

"Must have money to burn," muttered Marmaduke. "They live in that new house built on the paddock of the Pritchards' old place, don't they?"

"On Cedar Lane, yes," Aunt Beanie confirmed. "But of course they'd do anything for the safe return of their son."

Keya frowned. Malika had been reticent about paying the ransom money, and it looked as if she'd been proved right, and that the money hadn't been paid to the kidnapper. So why offer such a large reward now? Was she appealing directly to the person who'd taken her son?

"What are you thinking?" asked Aunt Beanie.

Keya stared at Nick's image on the TV as she replied, "That it's a large sum to offer as a reward."

"Did you notice that Nick said for the boy's safe return, not for information, which is what a reward is usually for?" Ryan said.

"What does that mean?" asked Monica.

"That the appeal is to the kidnapper," replied Norman. "Like a counter ransom offer."

Everyone was silent.

On the TV screen, Nick said, "That's all the information I have for now. Once again, I urge the public to be vigilant and call our help line," a number appeared on the bottom of the screen, "with any information they have regarding the missing boy."

Nick turned his back to the camera and walked steadfastly towards the front door.

Inspector Evans nodded at him, and they both entered the house.

"I hope I won't be put on phone duty," muttered Ryan as he cut a slice of chicken and pushed half a roast potato onto his fork.

"You're with me, and we have plenty to do," Keya reassured him.

"Does that mean you need help at the cafe next week?" asked Aunt Beanie hopefully.

"Possibly." Keya's voice was uncertain. The cafe was due to be closed on Monday, so if the case was concluded within the next 24 hours, she'd be there on Tuesday. Both her mum and Zivah were working next week, but with the cafe proving so popular perhaps there was too much work for Amma?

"Why don't you pop in on Tuesday morning and speak to my mum," Keya suggested. "See what she would like you to do?"

"Good idea. And I'll make a lemon drizzle cake to sell. We ran out of most cakes last week," Aunt Beanie explained.

"How's my grandson getting on?" asked Marmaduke. "Does he actually do anything?"

"Marmaduke!" Aunt Beanie chastised her brother.

"Thomas is doing really well. He started by making sandwiches, but I think he's now serving customers." Keya looked at Aunt Beanie for confirmation.

"He is, and he's really coming out of his shell," confirmed the older woman.

"It's so good for young people to have something else to do besides sit in their rooms on their computers. Although you did do a lot of that, Ryan." Monica looked lovingly at her son.

"I also played sport. And I taught computing and repaired equipment. In fact, I still do." Ryan smiled shyly.

"That's because the police pay you so little," said Monica, sounding rather prim.

"Actually, I enjoy it."

Marmaduke sipped his coffee, made a face, and placed his mug back on the table. He said, "I agree with you Monica. Which is why I'm paying young Olivia to do odd jobs for me. Since you wouldn't give her a job in the cafe."

"I'd love her to work for me," Keya said. "She's such a bright, personable girl, but she's under the legal employment age in Gloucestershire."

"What rubbish," muttered Marmaduke. "I had her mother and her sister working in the auction house and then the antique centre when they were young children. It never did them any harm."

"But you didn't pay them," pointed out Aunt Beanie dryly.

Marmaduke puffed out his chest and stared at his sister. "Well, it was better for them than hanging around at the lido, or on street corners, or worse still, holed up in their bedrooms. Who knows what young people get up to now?"

"Too true," sighed Aunt Beanie. "Pudding?" She looked at Keya and Ryan.

Ryan grinned and replied, "Yes, please."

CHAPTER TWENTY-FIVE

Keya placed her spoon in her empty dessert bowl and checked her watch. It was four o'clock on Sunday afternoon.

She looked across the large pine kitchen table at Aunt Beanie and said, "Thanks for a lovely lunch. The pasta was tasty, and I love fresh strawberries and raspberries at this time of year."

"With proper vanilla ice cream," Ryan added.

"But we better return to Cedar Lane and see what the inspector wants us to do next," Keya said.

She drove Ryan back to the Bartletts' in her VW Polo. She beeped several times at the entrance gate until a few reporters stepped out of her way.

Someone called, "That's Sergeant Varma. Oi, Sergeant, is Chief Inspector Greg coming back from his holidays to take over this case?"

Keya parked in the drive and, as she and Ryan climbed out of her car, Nick walked out of the front door and strode towards the pack of reporters.

He said evenly, "Chief Inspector Greg is currently taking some personal time."

'But surely this isn't an appropriate time to take a holiday?" the man who had recognised Keya shouted back.

"There is never a good time," Nick replied firmly, "But he will be kept informed of any updates in the case, and two very experienced inspectors are involved with it. Thank you."

Nick turned and walked back, meeting Keya and Ryan beside the front door. "I'm not sure how much longer I can hold them off without some real progress in the case," he confided. "Do you two have any leads?"

"Not really," said Keya as they entered the kitchen. "Plenty of hoaxes, as Chief Inspector Greg originally surmised, although we are following up on one which might be genuine."

"And what's that?" asked Inspector Evans.

He was leaning against the central kitchen island where Inspector Sue was sitting on a stool, a cup of coffee in front of her.

Her eyes looked tired, and when she looked up at Keya and smiled, Keya knew her heart wasn't in it. Had she been home? It looked as if the case was getting to her.

Keya told all three inspectors about the ransom letters that had been received and then about her trip to Cirencester with Ryan.

"You can use my team's equipment to look at the phone you found," Nick offered. "But what do you think you'll get from it?"

"Not much," Ryan accepted. "I suspect it was bought for the purpose of sending that message. But if that is the case, doesn't it show planning, forethought, and intent?"

"It certainly does," agreed Inspector Evans in a thoughtful tone. "The person who used the phone demanded £250,000 sent electronically. So if they still have the boy, why haven't they contacted the Bartletts again?"

"Perhaps they've been watching the house," suggested Inspector Sue, "And realised we've been focusing on another ransom demand. But if that's the case, they'll know by now that the money's been paid. So you're right. Why haven't they been in touch?"

She clasped her hands together on the counter and looked down at them.

Inspector Evans placed a hand on her shoulder. "Don't think the worst," he consoled. "There's still hope."

She looked up at him and asked dejectedly, "Is there?"

Wanting to change the subject, Keya asked, "The reward was a surprise. Especially the amount."

Inspector Evans was still regarding Inspector Sue with a concerned expression, so Nick replied, "We tried to talk Mrs Bartlett out of it, but she insisted."

"Quite a change from her reluctance to pay the original ransom sum," Keya remarked.

Nick nodded. "I agree. She didn't seem convinced about the original ransom money. But her son is still out there, and she does want him returned safely."

"Jonathan's beside himself with worry," said Inspector Sue.

"And guilt," added Keya.

"How is the nanny?" Ryan asked.

"She's locked herself in her room and won't come out. She blames herself for losing Zaad and the money, and she's convinced the Bartletts are going to sack her and send her home."

"Which they probably will do, after this is over," declared Inspector Evans. "But we mustn't get bogged down with worry. Look at that lass from Sussex. She turned up safe and sound this afternoon at a campsite in north Wales."

"That is a relief," agreed Inspector Sue.

"So, Ryan, you'll look at that mobile phone. Inspector Unwin, you and your team have your hands full, so Sergeant Varma, let's discuss any other line of enquires you've thought of. And I hope you have some, as I'm stumped."

Ryan followed Nick into the living room behind the kitchen.

Keya pulled out a stool and sat at the kitchen island facing Inspector Sue and Inspector Evans. She began, "Are we agreed that the balloon man was a hoax? And that he's run off with £48,000?"

"Unfortunately, yes," agreed Inspector Evans, "although I sent two constables into the town earlier to look for any signs of him, or anyone who might have seen him making his escape this morning."

Keya continued, "Ryan said the police officer who escorted Biljana here, after Zaad went missing, thought a boy on a bicycle delivered the first ransom note. It might be worth looking for him as he could be someone local that the balloon man found hanging around and paid to deliver the note."

"It's worth a shot, Dai," Inspector Sue said, looking up at Inspector Evans.

"It is. I'll call back those two constables and see if they can find the boy on the bike."

"Or girl. They were wearing a cycle helmet," Keya clarified.

"That might narrow it down. A lot of the kids don't wear helmets, despite your school road safety talks." Inspector Evans looked at Keya, who blushed.

"But, if we're agreed, and the balloon man is not the kidnapper, what leads do we have to find the real one?" asked Inspector Evans.

"What about the older sister?" suggested Keya.

"I've seen her at the cafe with the family, and I overheard that she'd recently left her husband. She doesn't have children of her own. Apparently she didn't want them, but the last time I saw her at the cafe, she was rather taken with little Zaad. She even offered to look after him. What if she decided she wanted a child after all, or that her sister wasn't a fit mother? Could she have run off with the toddler?"

Inspector Evans turned to Inspector Sue and asked, "Have we had any luck tracing Nadia Taylor?"

"No."

Inspector Evans stood taller and announced, "Then let's make finding her our priority."

CHAPTER TWENTY-SIX

Keya perched on the arm of a two-seater sofa in the small snug at the Bartletts' house. Malika was sitting on the sofa, and Inspector Sue was in the armchair.

Inspector Evans hadn't joined them, reasoning that Malika was more likely to open up to the two policewomen without him.

But he had suggested that Jonathan take a walk in the garden, and when Jonathan protested, Inspector Evans had insisted.

"Mrs Bartlett, do you know where your sister is?" Keya asked.

Malika gasped and blinked. Then she composed herself and said, "Nadia was here when I left for work yesterday morning. She didn't tell me she was leaving, but I presumed she'd gone back to her husband."

"My colleagues visited her house, and her husband hasn't seen her. He was relieved that she'd been staying with you, as she hadn't answered any of his calls or told him where she was. Do you have any idea where she might have gone?"

Malika sat back and crossed her arms. "No, but Nadia is an adult and quite capable of looking after herself. Surely, you should be concentrating on finding Zaad. Hasn't anyone come forward with any information yet?"

"Nothing credible, but it's Sunday afternoon, and people have …

other priorities. But I'm sure we'll hear something soon." Inspector Sue said in a reassuring tone.

Malika sniffed. "Nadia did have a close friend in Worcester. I think I have her details in an old address book."

"That would be useful. Thank you." Inspector Sue looked across at Keya.

Malika narrowed her eyes. "You don't think Nadia has anything to do with Zaad's disappearance, do you? She doesn't even like children."

"That's not entirely true, is it? She's rather taken to her nephew," Keya replied.

Malika stared out of the window and into the garden. "I'm certain she had nothing to do with it."

Keya heard a tap on the door leading into the corridor.

She stood up and opened it slowly.

Ryan whispered, "We've received another email."

"What is it?" called Malika, expectantly.

"I'm not sure. Will you excuse me?" Keya left the snug, closing the door behind her.

Neither she nor Ryan spoke until they were back in the kitchen.

Inspector Evans was waiting for them.

"At last, a breakthrough. Tell us all about it, Constable Jenkins."

"Nick, Inspector Unwin's team has continued to monitor the family's email address and other accounts. And they received another message from the email address DontTraceMe@gmail.com, which is the same address the sender used to send the email from the phone we found in Cirencester."

"The real kidnapper?" Inspector Evans looked hopeful.

"Perhaps," Ryan replied noncommittally.

"What did the email say?" asked Keya.

"It was along the lines of asking us if we'll now take them seriously, and that they still have Zaad. The boy enjoyed his fish fingers last night but refused to eat his peas until he had Mr Flopsy."

"Who's Mr Flopsy?" asked Keya in confusion.

"His toy rabbit," said Inspector Sue, joining them. "I'll ask Malika and Jonathan later about those details. Carry on. This sounds hopeful."

"Then the emailer said that, as we ignored their ransom demand, they will take the reward money instead. But as it's a Sunday, they will wait until tomorrow for the family to put the money together, and they'll be in touch with details of their Rebellion account."

Ryan stopped and looked at his senior police colleagues.

"This sounds real to me. The details. And following up the initial request," Inspector Sue stated.

"What do you suggest we do?" asked Inspector Evans.

"I'll speak to the Bartletts and tell them about the message and the request. But I think we'll all agree that, after that, there isn't much more any of us can do this evening. So if you don't mind, I'll ask a colleague from headquarters to take over while I try to get some sleep at home. I suggest you all go home, too."

Inspector Evans' phone rang.

He said, "I will, after I've updated the Chief Inspector. No doubt I'll need to persuade him for the umpteenth time not to come back, and that we have this under control. Which we do, don't we?" He looked round the group.

Keya, Inspector Sue, and Ryan all nodded, but Keya did not feel confident.

Inspector Evans answered his phone. "Yes, sir."

Inspector Sue picked up an overnight bag and said, "I'll come out with you and put this in my car, give myself time to think before I speak to the Bartletts."

She, Keya, and Ryan stepped outside into the drizzle. The sky had darkened with gathering clouds.

Keya stopped walking as a commotion began at the front gate. A car repeatedly beeped its horn. Surely the Chief Inspector hadn't abandoned his holiday plans already?

Gradually the crowd of reporters parted, although several camera lenses pointed at the windows of a black Mercedes, with a taxi sign on its roof, as it entered the driveway.

A rather bemused, but grinning Nadia climbed out, and the cameras clicked.

Inspector Sue strode towards her and demanded, "Are you Nadia? Do you have the boy?" She did not use her habitual motherly tone and the edge to her voice indicated the stress she was under.

Nadia stood taller and with her hand on the taxi door she

responded, "I am. But who are you? And what boy?"

Keya approached the taxi and said in a conciliatory tone, "Your sister and her husband are very upset. Zaad's missing and we wondered if you'd taken him away for a fun weekend?"

Nadia snorted. "I've certainly had a fun weekend, but not with a toddler."

The taxi driver had opened the boot, and he handed Nadia a small black wheeled suitcase.

As Nadia took it, she glanced back at the gate where the reporters pressed forward, probably trying to catch every word of the conversation. The young constable on duty was holding his arms out wide, but Keya wasn't sure how long he could hold back the tide.

The front door opened, and Malika ran out crying, "Nadia! Have you seen Zaad?"

Dragging her case across the gravel, Nadia moved towards her sister and said in a serious tone, "No, why would I? What about Ga..."

Malika cut her off. "He's gone, and we had to pay ransom money, but the man didn't even have Zaad."

"Now Malika," began Inspector Sue, "we don't know that, do we?"

Keya stepped back, surprised by the look of distaste on Malika's face as she addressed Inspector Sue. "I do. But you were the ones who insisted I pay that money. And now what? Where is my son?"

Nadia, who was standing in front of Malika, placed a hand on her sister's shoulder as she reassured her, "I'm sure Zaad's fine, and he'll soon come home."

Malika breathed in, trying to control herself, before she demanded, "Where have you been, Nadia?"

The older sister smiled conspiratorially as she replied airily, "To a little hotel in Bath. With your window cleaner."

Then Nadia turned back to the reporters, gave them a little wave, and walked into the house.

"Take a statement from the taxi driver," Inspector Sue instructed Ryan. "I better deal with Nadia's arrival." She sighed and returned to the house.

Standing out in the drizzle, Ryan asked, "Do you think she had anything to do with the boy's disappearance?"

"No," Keya replied. "She was playing an entirely different game."

CHAPTER TWENTY-SEVEN

On Monday morning, Keya once again picked Ryan up from Meadowbank Farm.

He appeared wearing a pair of brown moleskin trousers with a short-sleeved shirt and a lightweight black jacket draped over his arm.

Keya looked out of her windscreen. It did look like rain again.

As Ryan climbed into her car, she asked, "Why aren't you wearing your uniform?"

"Inspector Evans sent me a message and told me not to. I think he wants us following up leads today."

There was a bustle of activity when they reached the Bartletts' house. Reporters accosted them at the entrance gate again, but there were fewer than the evening before.

Inside the house, Inspector Sue was wearing a pair of yellow rubber gloves, and she was wiping down the kitchen surfaces.

"Next, she'll get the broom out and sweep us out with the trash," muttered Inspector Evans.

"Good idea," called Sue. "Keya, can you grab the broom from that cupboard over there and start sweeping?"

"Come on," Inspector Evans said to Ryan. "We need your help to set up a Rebellion account for Mrs Bartlett."

Ryan followed the inspector through to the living room as Keya started sweeping.

"I have a good feeling about today," remarked Inspector Sue in an upbeat voice. Clearly, she had slept well last night and was back in her supportive family liaison role.

"What happened after Nadia returned?" Keya asked.

"She and Jonathan had an enormous row, and she stormed out. I drove her to The Bull Hotel in Market Place."

"But did she know anything about Zaad being taken, or had she seen anything?"

"No, she was far too wrapped up in her own life and her naughty weekend away. I just hope that, if she does come back to this house, she'll be more sympathetic and supportive towards her sister. What did the taxi driver tell Ryan?"

Keya stopped sweeping. "Only that he had a call from the Z Hotel in Bath, from where he collected Nadia, and a man she called Dave, who he dropped off at the Eight Bells pub, before bringing Nadia here. Dave paid the fare with cash."

"So another dead end?"

"I'd say so. Even if someone was hanging around the house or the lane on Saturday morning, I doubt Nadia would have noticed them after what you said." Keya returned to sweeping the floor.

Just as she was tidying up the final pile of dust and dirt, Malika entered the kitchen. Her hair shone, and she was wearing a pair of tailored trousers and a cream blouse.

"You're not going to work, are you?" blurted Keya.

"No, but I want to be ready and alert today. And to bring my son home."

"That's the spirit. I'm sure we will," Inspector Sue agreed.

Inspector Evans appeared from the living room and said, "Mrs Bartlett. Excellent. Are you ready to set up your Rebellion account?"

Malika nodded. "I am."

The inspector ducked back into the room and then Ryan appeared, carrying a laptop, which he placed on the recently cleaned and disinfected central kitchen island.

"I've got as far as entering your family email address," said Ryan.

Malika joined him and pulled the laptop across in front of her. As she tapped keys, she said, "I'd rather use my personal address."

"OK, and now add a password."

Ryan turned away as Malika entered it.

"It wants double confirmation and my phone number," said Malika, continuing to type.

She removed her phone from her pocket and when it buzzed, she opened it, looked at the screen and tapped on the laptop keyboard. "That's all done," she said, pushing the laptop towards Ryan.

He turned back to face the island and checked through the setup on the computer. "Yes, it's done. Now we wait for the next message from the ..."

"The information we need to transfer the money," interjected Inspector Sue. "It is a large sum. Are you OK sending so much, and is it ready?"

Malika placed her hands on the top of the island and stared down at them as she said in a resolute voice. "It's a small price to pay for Zaad's safe return."

She looked up at Sue, and continued, "And yes, the bank liquidated my various investments and savings accounts, and the money is ready in my current account."

"You should transfer it to your Rebellion account once we've received instructions about where to send it on to," Ryan explained.

"I think I'll grab some fresh air." Malika picked up her phone and opened the French windows. Slipping her feet into a pair of pink crocs, she stepped outside.

Keya expected her to stare up at the grey sky or just breathe, but instead, Malika was engrossed in her phone. Did anyone live for the moment anymore?

"I better check on Biljana," said Inspector Sue, and Keya heard a door open.

After a few minutes in which Keya continued to stare out into the garden, she heard a phone ring. Turning round, she saw Ryan remove his phone from his trouser pocket.

He looked at the closed doors leading into the kitchen before answering, "Hi Ozzie, how are you?"

He waited for a reply.

"Yes, that was a relief. She was found in north Wales, wasn't she?"

Keya knew they were discussing the missing girl from Sussex, and it didn't take a genius to work out where the conversation was heading.

"I am, but I can't tell you anything about it. We're at a critical stage in the case."

Ozzie had asked Ryan about Zaad.

"Yes, I can confirm he is still missing."

"No, I can't say anything about a ransom."

He listened for longer this time.

"You know I'll let you have any information when I can, and thanks for the heads up on Ronnie Marsh, we'll look out for him. Bye."

"Who's Ronnie Marsh?" asked Keya when Ryan had finished the call.

"He's the journalist who's taken over from Ozzie at the Cirencester Times, and he's had quite a fall from grace. Ozzie said that he started at the Daily Mail and worked on exposing Robert Maxwell, the disgraced millionaire who stole from his pension funds and then died when he fell off his yacht."

"But that was years ago. Why has he ended up at the Cirencester Times?"

"I'd like to say he's helping out in a philanthropic way, but I doubt it. Ozzie said to watch out for him. He's been in trouble before for using unscrupulous ways to obtain information from the authorities."

Keya groaned. "Let's hope he's not interested in this case."

CHAPTER TWENTY-EIGHT

Keya waited by herself in the kitchen of the Bartletts house. She was sending an order to a local supplier of lettuces and vegetables when Inspector Evans entered the kitchen.

"Constable Jenkins just received an email from the kidnapper with instructions on when and where to send the money. Where is Mrs Bartlett?"

"I think she's still in the garden. What do the instructions say?"

"They give the number of an account and we've been told the money must be deposited at precisely 10.05 this morning."

Keya checked her black-strapped watch. "That's in twenty-five minutes."

"It is, so we all need to be alert. Before I find Mrs Bartlett, I want to give you your instructions. Constable Jenkins is currently trying to trace the IT address ..."

"I think you mean IP."

"That's what I said." Inspector Evans narrowed his eyes at her.

"Yes, sir. Sorry."

"If he does, I want you to go with him to find the location and, hopefully, the kidnapper. But don't spook them. Our priority is getting the boy back safely. Just follow the kidnapper, keep your distance, and don't try to apprehend them. Take your radio and your phone and we'll keep in touch."

"And if Ryan, PC Jenkins, doesn't trace the IP address."

Inspector Evans squared his shoulders. "I have every faith in him that he will. The boy's a genius."

Keya smiled and agreed, "He is."

"Inspector Sue and I will wait here with the family, and Inspector Nick's team will take over monitoring emails and incoming messages. Fingers crossed, we'll be given a location to find the boy."

The French windows opened, and Malika entered the kitchen. "Any news?" she asked, her tone practical rather than hopeful.

"Yes." Inspector Evans told her about the message.

"I need a cup of coffee, and then I'll work with your colleague to make the transfer," Malika said.

The kettle boiled and Malika poured hot water into a one-cup cafetiere. As she did, the living room door opened, and Ryan signalled to Inspector Evans.

Calmly, Malika poured out her coffee, added milk, and took her cup across to the central island.

Ryan and Inspector Evans reappeared, and the inspector nodded at Keya. But as Ryan moved towards the front door, Malika called out, "Where are you going?"

"Police work," replied Inspector Evans.

"But he can't go now. He has to help me."

Ryan drew his lips together and looked uncertainly at Inspector Evans.

The inspector considered the situation for a brief moment and then nodded.

Ryan carried his laptop across to the central island and said, "First, we need to transfer money from your personal account to your new Rebellion account."

Inspector Evans walked slowly down the kitchen towards the French windows and indicated with his head for Keya to join him.

"We're losing time," he muttered.

"Should I go without Constable Jenkins?" Keya asked.

The inspector glanced back at Ryan and Malika.

Ryan continued to give instructions.

"No, it might be dangerous. Once Ryan has set up the account, I'll ask him to show Sue what to do. Then she can make sure the money is transferred at the requisite time and you and Ryan can leave."

"What if Mrs Bartlett still protests?"

"She's a capable woman. All she needs is reassurance, and Sue can provide that."

Keya wasn't so sure Malika would be so understanding, but she was also conscious of the time ebbing away and that they would probably be too late now to find the kidnapper.

"And that's it," said Ryan. "All ready to go."

Inspector Evans crossed the kitchen and said, "Can you show Inspector Sue?"

"Sure," Ryan agreed.

Inspector Evans opened the door leading into the corridor and shouted, "Sue!"

A minute later, she appeared in the kitchen.

"Constable Jenkins has set up the transfer. I'd like him to show you what to do so you can assist Mrs Bartlett if needed, as I have another job for the constable."

"Oh, no!" protested Malika. "I need him."

"I'm sure I can help," Inspector Sue reassured her.

"Yes, it's very simple. All you need to do is log back in and click the send button," explained Ryan.

"But what if I forget my password?"

"Write it down," suggested Inspector Sue. "We won't look."

Inspector Evans handed Malika a pad from beside the phone and reluctantly she scribbled something on the second sheet.

"Very good. That's all set," announced Inspector Evans. "Sergeant Varma. Constable Jenkins. Keep in contact."

Keya knew it was her cue to leave.

"I need to grab another laptop," said Ryan. "I'll meet you outside."

CHAPTER TWENTY-NINE

"Where to?" Keya asked Ryan as she drove her car out of Cedar Lane.

"Back to Cirencester. This time to an area around Cricklade Street. I wasn't able to pinpoint the exact Wi-Fi network location."

Keya parked in her designated parking space at the side of Cirencester Police Station, but instead of entering the building, she and Ryan crossed the road and entered a narrow alley emerging onto Cricklade Street.

A number of high street brands still occupied premises in what had once been Cirencester's prime shopping street. But now they were interspaced by empty shops.

"Head towards the town centre," Ryan instructed.

After they'd walked another ten metres, he said, "I've got it. Bishop's Walk Shopping Centre. But the kidnapper was using the centre's Wi-Fi so they could be anywhere inside."

Keya picked up her pace as she checked her watch and cried, "On no. It's 10.07. We've probably missed them."

She and Ryan jogged up Cricklade Street and turned left, entering the shopping centre via an archway which had a 'Shops to Let' sign displayed above it.

There were only a handful of people in the small shopping centre and none of them were looking at their electronic devices.

"Where now?" asked Ryan.

Keya turned in a circle. "There," she cried. "My Moo."

They dashed across to the milkshake bar where four people were sitting outside on the L-shaped benches, separated from the main mall by two wooden planters filled with Yucca and other green-leafed house plants.

They stared at the customers, who ignored them. Two women chatted quietly while a teenage girl sucked on a pink and white straw. On the other side of the aisle, a youth wearing headphones scrolled through his phone.

"Is that him?" whispered Ryan.

"I don't know. Why don't you sit on the bench near him while I buy us both milkshakes?" suggested Keya. "What flavour would you like?"

Ryan consulted the wooden board protruding out of one of the planters. "Oh, I'll try a Terry's Chocolate Orange one."

Keya walked inside the bar as Ryan seated himself on the cushion bench, close to the headphone-wearing youth.

"Morning. What can I get you?" asked a blonde-haired girl with a tantalising smile. She was just the kind of waitress Keya would love for her cafe.

"A Chocolate Orange milkshake and," she hesitated and consulted the menu. She didn't want anything too sweet. "And an amaretto one."

"Regular or large?"

"Both regular."

"Any toppings?"

"No, thank you."

"That'll be £7.90. Are you paying by card?"

"Yes, and can I have a receipt?" Keya thought she could try to claim it on expenses. After all, they wouldn't be here but for the case.

"Quiet this morning," Keya said conversationally as she placed her card against the mobile reader.

"It's Monday morning," replied the girl.

Keya removed her warrant card and discreetly showed it to the girl, whose mouth opened in a silent 'oh'.

"Don't worry. All I'd like to know is how long that man with the headphones has been outside?"

"About ten minutes."

Keya checked her watch. It was nearly a quarter past ten. If he was the kidnapper, he'd need to have sent the message from elsewhere in the shopping centre.

"What other customers have you had this morning?" she asked the assistant.

"There have been several takeaways ..."

"No, people sitting down."

"Only one. A young woman wearing one of those black headscarves was already sitting outside with her laptop open when I arrived. I served her a milkshake, and she stayed until about five minutes ago."

"She was wearing a hijab?"

"I guess so, and a pair of large sunglasses, which was weird. I asked her if she was upset, as I thought she might be wearing them to cover up the fact she'd been crying, but she just nodded her head."

"How old would you say she was?"

"Mid-twenties, although it was hard to tell."

"Any accent?"

"Not really. She spoke softly and quietly, and she didn't want to chat. She just ordered a banana milkshake. But she did seem distracted, and keen to return to whatever she was doing on her computer. Anything else? Or shall I prepare your order?"

"That's all, thanks."

When Keya reappeared outside, having thanked the girl again for her help, she found Ryan sitting closer to the youth as they discussed a computer game.

Ryan stood when he saw her and said, "It's not Everett. He hasn't been here long. But he did say a girl wearing a hijab was busy on her laptop when he arrived. She didn't say anything and left just before we came."

"The assistant at the counter said the same thing. And that the young woman was wearing large sunglasses and barely spoke. She was already here when the assistant arrived to open up."

Ryan took the pink and white striped milkshake container and stepped into the mall. He consulted the menu. "Opening time was 9.30. Do you think the woman was our kidnapper?"

"One of them, perhaps. The mall will have CCTV footage, but I doubt it'll tell us any more about her. She clearly didn't want to be seen."

"You mean the hijab and sunglasses were a disguise?"

"Exactly."

Sucking on the straws of their milkshakes, they walked out of the shopping centre.

CHAPTER THIRTY

"Yes, sir," said Keya, speaking to Inspector Evans on her phone.

The inspector instructed, "And stay in Cirencester for the moment while we wait to hear about the boy. But tell Constable Jenkins to be ready to trace the email if, and when, it arrives."

"Yes, sir," Keya repeated before finishing the call.

She and Ryan were leaning against the black railings enclosing The Forum car park, facing the entrance to Cirencester Police Station.

She stood up, turned to Ryan, and said, "Your colleagues tracked the money, but it left the kidnapper's Rebellion account soon after it arrived. We have no idea where it is now."

"That was clever of the kidnapper," reasoned Ryan, "but we still might be able to trace it. So what now? Back to Fairford?"

"No, the inspector asked us to stay here and," Keya checked her watch, "I fancy a trip to Waitrose."

"Now? Can't your shopping wait?"

Keya stepped back, eyeing Ryan. "Do you really think I can afford to buy my weekly shop from Waitrose? No, I thought we could see if anyone turns up for a bag of pretend money, as per that ransom email sent to Corinium Radio."

"Oh, I get you." Ryan grinned. "But we will need a Waitrose carrier bag."

Keya started walking towards her car. She said, "So I'll treat you to lunch. Not bad, considering you've already had a milkshake this morning."

Ryan followed.

"How was it? The milkshake," she asked.

"Different, but sweet. I think I'll stick to fruit next time."

A large Waitrose supermarket was located on the northern edge of Cirencester. As they drove steadily around the car park, Keya peered out of her windscreen and asked, "Can you see the sign for row K?"

She turned into the next row and Ryan called out, "There, ahead of us."

"Read out the instructions again from that email. Not the money bit, but where the bag is to be dropped."

Ryan read, "In a Waitrose shopping bag left in the dustbin by the trolley shelter in row K."

"This is the trolley shelter." Keya slowed down.

"And that's the dustbin," Ryan added.

He and Keya both turned to look out of the driver's window at an open-topped green plastic rubbish bin.

Keya drove slowly forward and considered, "Our would-be ransom taker will need to see the dustbin, so they'll probably park in the row behind and to the right. That'll give them the best view, although, at the moment, there are plenty of empty spaces back here.

"I think I'll go back round and park on the other side of the shelter, but in sight of the bin. Then you can check your laptop for updates while I buy lunch and get us a shopping bag."

Keya approached the supermarket, which sold high quality, and highly priced products but also some unusual ingredients which she sometimes came in search of. When she did, she usually treated herself to something tasty from the discount use-by-today section.

She also remembered attending the store a few years ago as a constable, when a gang had ram-raided one of the front windows and stolen a freestanding cash machine from inside the store.

It turned out to be one of many such raids across the country undertaken by a gang who wore black balaclavas. They'd hadn't found the gang, the cash machine, or the money.

She bought a pack of steak and caramelised onion sandwiches for Ryan, and a feta crumb and lemon quinoa salad for herself.

Using the self-service checkout machine, she was asked how many bags she'd used. She tapped one and took a plastic bag with the store name on from a bunch hanging beside the machine.

She also collected her receipt. She'd be pushing it to claim lunch as well as the milkshakes, but it was certainly worth a try.

She also needed something to stuff in the bag, to make it look like it contained cash. Walking up and down the area behind the main checkout tills, she found a collection of cardboard boxes for shoppers to use.

Inside one there were some crumpled up balls of tissue paper. Perfect. She collected as many as she could and added them to the lunch items in the bag. Then she carried everything back to her car.

Slipping into the driver's seat, she checked her watch. "Our deposit window opens in ten minutes," she told Ryan as she handed him his brown paper bag of sandwiches.

"Thanks," said Ryan, starting to open the bag.

"Not now. They're for later. Any news from the kidnapper?"

"Nothing yet," Ryan said, in a disgruntled tone.

Keya removed her salad, placed it on the back seat, and rearranged the tissue paper inside the bag.

"It doesn't look very full," remarked Ryan.

"Well it's the best I can do. Five minutes. Let's see what cars arrive. Or perhaps the person is already here, waiting."

Looking past Ryan, she noted five other cars in the row. A Range Rover and another grey 4x4 were parked at the far end. A silver estate was two spaces away and, beyond it, two smaller cars.

A white one she thought was a Toyota Yaris, and the other a battered blue Ford Fiesta. None of them had anyone sitting in them, as far as she could see.

As they waited, Ryan kept tapping keys on his laptop, but Keya refrained from asking him what he was doing. She also resisted the urge to jump out of her car at precisely eleven o'clock and instead, she continued to watch the parking lot.

A mother pushed a laden shopping trolley across the car park with a young child sitting in the front of it, facing her. She stopped beside the Range Rover and began unpacking her groceries.

Keya waited until the lady finished and pushed her trolley to the collection bay. When she removed her child from the trolley and began walking back to her car, Keya said, "I'm going now. Keep a lookout for anyone approaching the trolley bay and dustbin."

Ryan folded his laptop away as Keya climbed out of the car. Trying to act casually, she strode towards the trolley bay and carefully placed the Waitrose shopping bag in the bin, on top of an empty McDonald's drink container.

Unhurriedly, she returned to her car, resisting the temptation to look into the parked cars.

"Should we drive away?" Ryan asked.

"Oh Toda! I hadn't thought of that. Nobody's going to approach the bin while I'm still here." Keya looked around. "I'll tell you what. I'll drive away, but I'll stop behind that white van over there so you can climb out. Then you can watch the bin while I find somewhere else to park, out of sight."

"OK," Ryan agreed.

Keya drove off, deposited Ryan beside the white van, and found a space on the other side of the car park. Ducking behind cars, she made her way back to row K.

Glancing up over the roof of a Suzuki Vitara, she spotted a man wearing a flat cap sloping towards the shopping trolley bay. His hands were stuffed into the pockets of his blue padded gilet and his shoulders and head were bent. He looked like someone who didn't want to be recognised.

Glancing back at the white van, she could see that Ryan had also seen the man. Ryan was peering around the side of the vehicle, and she could tell he was itching to move.

"Wait," she murmured to herself. "Steady."

The man reached the trolley bay and proceeded straight to the dustbin, lifting the bag out of it.

He looked inside and Keya heard his angry shout. "No!"

She ran round the car towards the trolley bay, but Ryan was quicker, and before the man reached his battered blue Ford Fiesta, Ryan wrapped his arms around him and nearly lifted him off his feet.

"Good work, Constable," said Keya breathlessly.

"Let me go," shouted the man. "I'm a journalist."

"So what?" rebuked Keya. "You still tried to extort money illegally."

"It was a trap. To see if the incompetent local police force would follow up leads on the kidnapping," said the man, struggling in vain against Ryan's grip.

"This police force has plenty to do looking for a missing boy without wasting our time on hoaxes." Keya's voice rose in anger.

"Then why are you here?" cried the man. He was in his sixties with strands of grey hair poking out from under his cap. And his face was sallow, with dark hollows under his eyes.

"Because we were in the area. And I hate those who take advantage of other people's pain and suffering," Keya answered. Then she said to Ryan, "Let him go."

Ryan eyed her for confirmation before easing his grip, but he still looked ready to pounce should the man try to escape.

Instead, the man pulled a wallet out of the pocket of his gilet and said, "See. Press."

Keya leaned forward and read the name on the press pass. "Ronnie Marsh. We've been warned about you." She looked up at the surprised journalist, grinning.

"You have?"

"Yes, and I wonder what we should charge him with, Constable Jenkins? Wasting police time? Extortion? Attempted theft?"

"Please, please. I didn't mean any harm. It was just a ..."

"Just a joke," exclaimed Ryan. "A young boy is missing. How is that a joke?"

"That isn't what I meant," muttered Ronnie.

Keya's phone rang in her pocket. Removing it, she saw Inspector Evans' name. Stepping away from Ryan and the still protesting journalist, she answered, "Yes, sir."

"The kidnapper phoned. The boy's been left at a cafe. Your cafe."

"But it's not open today."

"Then you better head straight over, and I'll meet you there."

"Yes, sir."

Hastily, she shoved her phone back into her pocket and called to Ryan. "Leave him. We have somewhere else to be."

"Is this about the boy?" enquired Ronnie, his seasoned journalistic nose probably sniffing a lead.

"If it was, I wouldn't tell you. And if I see you anywhere near the family, their house, or this case, I'll arrest you for … something."

Keya jogged back to her car, and she'd already turned the engine on by the time Ryan climbed in.

They drove past Ronnie, who watched them leave with a calculating expression.

Keya knew she hadn't seen the last of him, but once again, bringing Zaad safely home was her main concern.

At the junction leaving the supermarket, she pressed down hard on the accelerator.

The car behind her blared its horn as she shot out determinedly into the traffic, heading towards Akemans.

CHAPTER THIRTY-ONE

"Are we going to find Zaad?" asked Ryan, gripping the grab handle above the car door as Keya leaned to the right and accelerated hard out of the bend.

"Yes. That was Inspector Evans on the phone. Someone called and said the boy's been left at my cafe, but it's Monday and we're closed."

"Oops," Ryan replied.

"Can you call Gilly Wimsey and ask her to look out for him?"

"I can, but only if you slow down."

Keya eased off the accelerator and drove smoothly through a left bend.

"Thank you." Ryan sounded grateful as he removed his phone from his pocket.

Keya heard Gilly answer and ask, "Any news of that missing boy?"

"Yes," replied Ryan. "We've received a call that he's going to be left at Akemans. Actually, at the cafe, but as that's closed, he may be abandoned in the antique centre, or somewhere nearby. We're on our way, but can you keep an eye out for him?"

"I'm in my office, but I'll go downstairs immediately. What does he look like?"

"Dark-haired, olive-coloured skin."

"Mr Flopsy," Keya prompted.

"Oh, yes," added Ryan. "And he'll probably be carrying a toy rabbit."

"Right. Leave it with me and I'll see you soon."

Gravel sprayed out from under Keya's wheels as she braked sharply to a stop in Akemans car park. She thought she spotted Nick's metallic grey Mercedes. Had he driven Inspector Evans?

Without waiting for Ryan, or locking her car, Keya dodged around vehicles and ran towards the wooden entrance door of the antique centre.

Inside, Nick and the inspector were surveying the large space. Keya didn't stop to speak to them but sprinted between two rows of stalls. Surprised shoppers jumped back, out of her way. Approaching the back of the centre, and the closed entrance to the cafe, she slowed down.

She thought she heard a girl's voice.

Emerging from between the stalls, she saw Olivia, Gilly's daughter, holding out a piece of chocolate to a tearful looking toddler.

"Olivia?" called Keya, gently.

Olivia looked up and smiled.

The boy took the piece of chocolate as Olivia said, "Yes, this is Zaad."

Slowly, Keya approached Olivia and Zaad. She said in a soothing voice, "Hi, Zaad."

The boy, who now had chocolate smeared around his mouth, giggled and held up his rabbit. "Gami."

"Is that the name of your rabbit?" Keya thought it was Mr Flopsy, but she decided to play along.

"Gami," the boy repeated.

"He's been saying that since I found him," explained Olivia.

"Good Gami," said Keya. "Would you like to go home?"

The little boy's eyes widened, and he nodded.

"Why don't you escort him, Olivia, since you found him?"

Olivia held out her hand, and Zaad wrapped his smaller one around her fingers as she led him between the rows of stalls, back towards the entrance.

People stopped talking as they passed, and someone asked Keya, "Is that the missing boy?"

Keya nodded, and she heard the whispers start behind her as she followed Olivia and Zaad.

"Oh well done, Livy," exclaimed Gilly, rushing towards them. She scooped the little boy up in her arms and he gurgled in delight.

"Is that him?" Nick said, stepping into the space at the end of the row.

"Of course it is, and he's absolutely fine." Gilly smiled indulgently at Zaad.

"I believe it is, sir." Keya felt strange calling Nick sir, as, until recently, he'd been a sergeant, just like her.

"At last," announced Inspector Evans, his voice loud but full of relief. "Did you find him, lass?" The inspector addressed Olivia, who nodded her head.

"Well, you better come with me and Inspector Nick, and bring the boy. And your mother?"

Gilly exclaimed, "Oh yes, I'll come too. I just need to let Aunt Beanie know I'll be away for a while."

Nick led Olivia, Zaad, and Gilly, who was speaking on her phone, out of the antique centre.

"That's that, sir," said Ryan when he joined Keya and Inspector Evans at the front of the antique centre. Many of the customers were still staring at them.

"Not exactly," grunted the inspector.

"We have the boy back and that's the main thing, but a crime has still been committed. Two, if you count the balloon man's 'theft' of £48,000. So what I want you two to do is question the stall holders and any of the customers who saw the boy, or, in particular, anyone with him."

"Yes, sir," chorused Keya and Ryan.

"Call me when you're finished, and we'll decide what to do next. I don't want to crowd the family, but I would like to know if there's anything the boy can tell us. Inspector Sue should be able to help with that."

CHAPTER THIRTY-TWO

As Inspector Evans left the antique centre, Ryan turned to Keya and asked, "Where should we start our interviews?"

Keya considered, "The kidnapper thought the cafe was open. To reach it, they'd have to walk through the antique centre. What route would they choose?"

Ryan walked across to the wooden entrance doors and looked towards the stalls.

Then he returned to Keya and said, "Either along that avenue," he pointed to the second one from the right, "or they'd avoid as many stalls as possible by taking the route along the side wall."

"OK, let's start by the wall, as there's only one row of stalls. I'll take the corner homeware booth and you speak to the person manning the stall next to it."

The homeware stall was stylishly laid out, like a photograph in a magazine. It was painted white, and strings of fairy lights zigzagged across the top.

A high-level shelf held coloured glass vases and lamps with an assortment of attractive shades. In the corner, a ladder-type shelving unit displayed pastel-coloured cushions and throws.

"Can I help you?" asked a very thin lady wearing a pair of white jeans. Her voice had an upper-class tone of superiority.

"I hope so." Keya help up her warrant card in its black wallet and said, "A young boy was found in the centre earlier. We're looking for the person who brought him here."

"I've no idea. I don't allow children on my stall."

Deciding the woman couldn't tell her anything useful, Keya said a polite, "Thank you."

She and Ryan made their way down the row interviewing stall holders, but none of them remembered seeing Zaad or his companion.

Reaching the far end, near the closed door of the cafe, Keya declared, "Let's try the second avenue you pointed out and see if we have better luck there."

Once again, Keya spoke to the first stallholder and Ryan to the next one up.

"Oh yes, the young boy Olivia found," said the elderly man. "She's a good kid. I heard her call out and when I looked up, she was approaching the toddler who was just standing by the door to your cafe."

"Was the boy on his own?"

"He appeared to be, but someone must have left him there. He didn't look like the type to just wander off, but you never know."

The man smiled sadly at Keya and added, "By the way, I wanted to thank you. Takings at my stall have tripled since you opened your cafe." He winked at her. "So I treat myself on an afternoon to a cappuccino and a piece of cake."

"Oh, I'm so glad," said Keya. "And you do know that as a stallholder you receive a discount?"

"No, I didn't."

"Keya," called Ryan.

"Excuse me." Keya moved to the next stall.

Ryan stood beside a tall lady with dark wavy hair and when Keya appeared he said to the woman, "Please can you repeat what you told me?"

"Of course," the woman replied primly.

"I looked up from my desk and saw an Arab woman dragging a young boy towards the back of the centre. He was crying. Then Rozie, next door, who's looking after her aunt's stall, ran after the boy with a teddy or something, which calmed him down. And that's all I saw."

Keya nodded. "When you say Arab woman, what do you mean?"

"Well she had on one of those black headscarves."

"Just a black headscarf, or was she wearing a black burka?" pressed Keya.

"Oh, you mean one of those dress type things. No, I would have noticed that. I think her clothes were … normal."

"Is there anything else you can tell us about her? Her height, weight, or the way she spoke?"

"I didn't hear her say anything, and she was, well, as I said, normal. Why don't you speak to Rozie? She might know more."

Keya and Ryan thanked the woman and moved on to the next stall, which sold a variety of what Keya considered vintage rather than antique items. Ryan squatted down to examine a tower for an old desktop computer.

"Can you believe my phone has more processing power than that cumbersome thing?" said a teenage girl.

"These towers still have useful parts in them," Ryan replied, standing up, "And that was state-of-the art at the time."

The girl gave Ryan a typical teenage 'whatever' shrug.

"I understand you rescued a boy's teddy earlier," said Keya conversationally as she picked up a delicate floral painted milk jug.

"It was a rabbit, not a bear, and so what if I did?"

"That boy was the one who's been on the news. He's been missing for two days," said Keya.

"Really!" This information finally interested the girl. "But wasn't that his sister with him? Wearing the hijab?"

"Why would you think that?"

"Well she was young. Not my age, but not as old as you."

Keya ignored the possibly unintentional insult and said, "We think she was connected to the kidnappers."

"No way."

"Did you speak to her?"

"No, but when I gave the boy his toy rabbit, she said 'thanks', and then she tugged his arm and said, 'Come on'."

"Was the girl thin, or did she have a fuller figure, and what about an accent?" Keya tried to keep her voice casual and instead of looking at the girl, she picked up a wooden box.

"She was slim, and she was wearing a pair of violet Converse trainers. I don't remember an accent."

"So you gave the boy the rabbit and then?" Keya asked.

"I turned back to my aunt's stall. Two women had stopped in front of it and were looking at those baskets." She pointed to a small collection of shopping bags and baskets at the corner of the stall, including a red and cream checked one with a leather handle.

"And did you see the boy or woman again?"

The teenager shook her head.

"Thank you for your help."

"What do you think?" whispered Ryan. "The same woman who was in the milkshake cafe?"

"It sounds like it. We now know she was youngish, slim, of average height, and with no discernible accent. And she wears a pair of violet converse trainers. It's not much to go on, but it's a start."

None of the other stallholders could add anything about the mystery woman, so when Keya and Ryan returned to the entrance of the antique centre, Keya called Inspector Evans.

"We haven't learned anything from the boy," the inspector informed Keya.

"His mother whisked him away as soon as he returned, and she's refusing to let him speak to us. His father can't stop thanking us for finding him, and he seems completely oblivious to the fact that his wife paid nearly a quarter of a million pounds for the boy's safe return."

"And the nanny?" asked Keya.

"Still crying."

"In relief, I hope," said Keya.

"That's what Sue says. Can you and Ryan come and collect Mrs Wimsey and her daughter and drop them back at Akemans. Inspector Onion has briefed the press, and his team will be packing up when they've finished sending out updates. I'm not sure there's much more we can do here today," the inspector concluded.

"Where now?" asked Ryan when Keya finished the call.

"Back to Cedar Lane."

CHAPTER THIRTY-THREE

As Keya approached the turning to Cedar Lane in Fairford, she spotted a group of teenage kids standing on the pavements, holding onto bicycles.

"Slow down," Ryan instructed. "I want to see if they'll talk to me. Park just after that lamppost and I'll get out."

Keya braked gently to a stop, a couple of metres in front of the group of seven or eight boys. She noticed that none of them were wearing cycle helmets.

They turned to look at Ryan as he climbed out of her car, and they continued to watch him as he walked casually towards them.

Keya wondered what she'd do if they jumped on their bikes and sped off? Chase them? But they'd know all the twists and turns, and the alleys where she couldn't drive a car.

A blonde-haired boy puffed out his chest as Ryan approached and instinctively, Ryan stopped and addressed him.

Keya lowered her car window, hoping to catch part of the conversation.

"No man, we didn't go to the match on Saturday," said the blonde-haired boy.

"My dad said he'll take me to the rematch," called a ginger-haired boy from the back of the group.

"When's that?" asked Ryan.

"Week tomorrow."

"Do you think Fairford will win?"

"Course they will," chorused the boys. "Hey, are you a fan or not?"

"I follow Cheltenham Albion, but I've been to a few of Fairford's matches since I moved here."

This comment was followed by several unrepeatable remarks about the Cheltenham football team.

"Look, were you guys hanging around here before the match last Saturday, around lunchtime?"

"Naw, I was home."

"Course you were, Scotty. Stuffing your face."

Several other comments were directed at the ginger-haired boy, whose face reddened.

Ryan pressed on. "Did a man approach you wanting a job done?"

"What sort of job?" asked the blonde-haired boy.

"A delivery. In particular, a letter."

"No, we ain't no postie."

"What about that geezer wearing the Villa shirt?" shouted out another boy.

"Him. We sent him packing," replied the blonde-haired boy.

Several of the boys jeered in support.

"What did the man in the Villa shirt look like?" Ryan asked.

"He thought himself tough, he did. Had loads of tats on his arms. Hey, what's it to do with you, anyway? Are you police or summit?"

"Yeah, he's the filth," a tall boy at the back shouted and he spun round, jumped on his bike, and pedalled away.

Other boys followed his lead.

The blond-haired boy stepped closer to Ryan and smirked at him before also climbing on his bike and riding away.

Ryan didn't move. He just stared after them.

Then Keya heard shouting and one boy detached himself from the group and pedalled back to Ryan. It was the ginger-haired boy.

"Look, mister. I don't want any trouble. None of us delivered a letter, but when I came back from lunch, I saw Jess turn into Cedar Lane, and I think she was carrying a letter."

Keya couldn't hear the rest of the conversation as the boy and then

Ryan lowered their voices. She waited impatiently, tapping her steering wheel, for Ryan to return to the car.

When he did, he opened the car door and said, "We have a lead. Jessica Daniels. She's staying with her grandparents at the second house in the lane. I'll walk there in case she's riding around on her bike."

Keya gave Ryan a head start and messaged Inspector Evans to let him know she and Ryan were on their way but following up a lead first.

The hedge fronting the lane was completely overgrown and Keya nearly missed the entrance to the second house along. A wooden gate was ajar - perhaps Ryan had opened it for her - so she drove carefully through.

The house was actually a stone bungalow, set in several acres of well-tended garden. Beside the garage, whose rollover shutter door was raised, a teenager was tending to an upturned bicycle.

Ryan started talking to the figure as Keya climbed out of the car. Closer up, she realised it was a girl with a short bob of brown hair. Jessica Daniels, she presumed.

Ryan said to Jessica, "No, you're not in any trouble. But my colleague and I are trying to trace a man who gave you a letter to deliver on Saturday."

"I don't know anything about a letter," said Jessica as she picked up a tool and started levering the tyre off her bike.

"Sure you do," said Keya, approaching her. "How much did he give you to deliver it?"

Jessica stopped working on the bike and looked up at Keya with large, worried eyes. "Look, I had no idea the boy was missing. I just took the £5 and delivered the letter. How was I to know it was from the kidnapper?"

"It wasn't from the kidnapper," said Keya levelly.

"It wasn't?"

Keya explained, "We think someone local realised what had happened, and they took advantage of the situation by demanding money from the family. You did nothing wrong."

Jessica breathed out in relief.

Keya continued, "But we are trying to find the man because what he did was illegal."

"Oh."

"Can you tell us what he looked like?"

"Sure. He was bald, well his head was shaved, and he was wearing an Aston Villa football shirt and had tattoos on his arms."

"Had you seen him before?"

"No, but Dad only dropped me off here on Friday evening. I live in Banbury. But the man might have been in church on Sunday. My gran dragged me there, but I was bored and listened to music most of the time."

"The organ."

"What? No, my phone." She grinned. "Gran says I'm as deaf as Grandad, but she doesn't realise I have my EarPods in." Jessica lifted up her hair and Keya spotted the white plastic device in her ear.

"Is that all?" Jessica asked. "Just I need to mend my puncture before I rejoin the boys."

"Thank you. That was very helpful. And the little boy has been returned to his parents." Keya climbed back into her car and drove down to the Bartletts' house while Ryan walked, closing the gate behind her.

Three journalists were still standing outside the Bartletts' entrance gate. They stared at Keya in a bored manner before returning to their phones.

When Keya entered the kitchen, she found Gilly Wimsey and Inspector Sue sitting at the central island, drinking tea. The patio doors were open, and she heard laughing voices outside.

"Back to normal," she commented.

"I'm not sure," mused Inspector Sue.

"It wouldn't surprise me if this house is on the market in a few weeks. I think this incident has brought home to Malika the importance of spending time with her son, rather than always being at work. And earning pots of money is not the key to happiness."

"I agree with that sentiment," said Gilly. "At times it's been hand to mouth in our family, but we have each other and I wouldn't miss the moments I've had with my kids. Listen to Olivia now. She's having a wonderful time playing with Zaad. But she's already changing. More and more it's about make-up, her image, and boys."

She looked at Keya. "Perhaps not a stage in life that bothered you?"

Keya frowned. "I did try make-up, and nightclubs and all that, but it wasn't for me. Anyway, like a typical Indian family, my parents made sure I studied hard. And it paid off."

"What did?" asked Ryan as he entered the kitchen.

"Studying. Now we should find the inspector and tell him about our enquiries into the balloon man," said Keya.

"He's in the living room talking to Nick. The media team has packed up and most of them have left."

Keya and Ryan entered the room behind the kitchen. It was the first time Keya had been in it. The sofa and chairs were pushed to the edges of the room and she presumed, by the marks on the carpet, that the media team had set up tables to work on in the middle of the room.

"We're nearly finished here," said Inspector Evans when they walked in.

"Inspector Unwin has completed his press briefings, and we won't get any more out of the family for the moment. What was the lead you were following up?"

Keya and Ryan explained about the kids on their bikes and the man who'd given Jessica the envelope.

"That's good work, and something to follow up tomorrow. Can you take Mrs Wimsey and her daughter back and I'll see you both at the station for a briefing at, let's say, half past eight in the morning?"

CHAPTER THIRTY-FOUR

Gilly climbed into the back of Keya's car and lifted up a plastic salad container.

"My lunch," Keya explained. "I haven't had time to eat it."

"I know. I should have eaten my sandwiches earlier." Ryan gave Keya a pained look before folding himself into the passenger seat.

Olivia jumped into the back beside Gilly, who said, "We'll get out at Meadowbank Farm when you drop Ryan off. Peter can pick us up and I need to speak to Aunt Beanie."

Keya drove back over the stone bridge with the River Coln flowing beneath it and turned into the entrance of Meadowbank Farm.

"That's Mum's car," cried Ryan as Keya parked next to a pale blue Toyota estate. "I hope everything's OK."

He jumped out and hurried up the path, followed by Gilly and Olivia.

Keya picked up the paper packet containing Ryan's beef sandwiches and reached into the back for her salad. Luckily, the weather hadn't been too warm today so the salad might still be edible.

In the farmhouse kitchen she found Monica reassuring Ryan, "I just popped round with some clippings for Beanie's garden. But I hear you found the boy."

"I did," cried Olivia.

And while Ryan, Gilly and Olivia told Monica, Aunt Beanie and Norman about the case, Keya placed a battered chrome kettle on the hottest plate of the AGA cooker and waited for it to boil.

"Whose is this lunch?" asked Aunt Beanie.

"Mine and Ryan's. We haven't had time to eat it."

Aunt Beanie removed two mismatched china plates from a cupboard and set them down on the wooden counter. Then she instructed Keya, "Sit down and eat. I'll bring you a cup of tea when it's ready. In fact, I'll make us all one."

Keya sat down wearily at the table next to Norman. The others were still standing and discussing the case.

"A relief to have the boy back, but how much did it cost the family?" asked Norman.

"£48,000 in cash to the man who took the rucksack from the church, and another £200,000 sent electronically."

Norman whistled.

As Keya tipped her salad onto her plate, he said, "Not everyone has that amount lying around. How did the kidnapper know?"

Keya chewed on her salad, thinking through Norman's question.

"The demand was never more than £250,000. The balloon man. That's what we call the man from the church as he left a red balloon with his note on Sunday morning, asked for £48,000, which we all agreed is a very precise amount."

"Anything strike you about that figure?"

"It's not enough to buy a two-year-old Porsche Cayenne," mused Keya.

"Eh?"

"It was the amount in their savings account. I overheard Malika in the cafe saying it was for her son's education."

"Who else knew about that?"

"Her family. The nanny. And anyone else who, like me, overheard her discussing it."

"So it doesn't exactly narrow things down?"

Keya slowly shook her head. "No."

"And the remaining money. Who knew about that?"

"A lot of people, including you, knew they'd bought that expensive new house on Cedar Lane. And then it was Malika Bartlett herself who offered the £200,000 as a reward."

"I always say follow the money, but I'm not sure how that's going to help you with this case," Norman conceded.

"If Ryan or the team in Gloucester can trace the electronic transfer, it might. But the kidnappers knew what they were doing. They immediately transferred the money out of the account the Bartletts sent it to, and who knows how many other accounts it has passed through since then."

"So what next?" asked Norman.

"We'll still try to track down those who kidnapped young Zaad and extorted money from the Bartletts. Talking of which, do you know a journalist called Ronnie Marsh?"

Norman flinched, and his eyes turned cold.

"Here you are. Tea. And would you like a piece of carrot cake? Monica brought it with her."

The shadow which had passed across Norman's face retreated and he smiled up at Aunt Beanie. "Thanks. A small slice would be nice."

Keya looked up at Aunt Beanie and asked, "Did you see a shaven-headed man at church on Sunday? One with tattoos."

Aunt Beanie looked puzzled. Then she said to Norman, "What about Susan William's son, Jason? His head is shaved, and he brought his mum to the service on Sunday."

"Does he have tattoos?" asked Norman.

"I've no idea. He usually wears a casual black jacket."

"Do you know where I can find him?" asked Keya.

"I think he moved back into the extension above his mum's garage on Moor Lane, at the southern end of Fairford."

Keya finished her salad as Aunt Beanie placed two slices of cake in front of her and Norman. For a fleeting moment, she tried to resist, and then she picked up her fork and used it to cut into the moist brown cake with frosted cream icing.

"Delicious!"

Ryan, Gilly, and Monica stopped talking.

"Do you think so?" asked Monica.

"I certainly do."

"Good enough to serve in your cafe."

Keya hesitated, sensing a trap.

Ryan jumped in. "Mum's been begging me to ask you if she can bake for the cafe, but with everything you've had on, I haven't found the right time to ask."

"I certainly think customers would enjoy it," Aunt Beanie said, standing holding her plate. "What do you think, Olivia?"

Olivia nodded, her mouth full.

"It's not that. I just need to check with Zivah and my mum that they're happy with new suppliers."

"I'll take a slice of Monica's cake with me tomorrow when I go to see your mum," Aunt Beanie suggested.

"Mum's great at pastry too," Ryan added proudly. "No soggy bottoms."

"As I said, let me think about it and speak to Amma and Zivah. But this really is delicious." Keya returned to her carrot cake.

As she sipped her tea, her appetite satisfied, she checked her watch. A quarter past four. She and Ryan had time for one more visit today.

"Ryan, if you're finished, I think we should pay Jason Williams a visit."

"Who's he?" asked Ryan.

"He might just be our shaven-headed tattooed balloon man. Aunt Beanie saw him in church on Sunday, and he lives with his mum in Fairford."

"That all fits."

Keya and Ryan followed Aunt Beanie's directions, simplified by Norman, to a housing estate built on the southern edge of Fairford in the 1970s. The houses stood in larger plots than most modern estates and were a variety of detached and semi-detached houses and bungalows.

"I think this is the one," Ryan said as Keya drove slowly down the street. "There's an extension over the garage, which could be where Jason lives."

Keya pulled to a stop and she and Ryan climbed out and walked up to the front door. Keya pressed the black plastic doorbell.

"Don't rush me, I'm coming," an elderly female voice called from inside.

Keya and Ryan waited patiently until the door opened and a

stooped woman, leaning on a stick, said, "Sorry, I'm not that quick on my feet these days."

Her words were unclear as her false teeth were missing.

"Are you Mrs Williams, and do you have a son called Jason?"

"He's not done anything wrong. He's a good boy."

"I'm sure he is," Keya placated her. "He took you to church on Sunday."

"That he did." Mrs Williams sounded less hostile. "But he's not home at the moment. Villa is playing away."

Which didn't mean much to Keya, expect that Jason wouldn't be back until much later, and he was unlikely to be sober.

"Thank you. We'll call again in the morning." Keya wanted to add, please don't tell him we called, but she knew that would only make the old lady more suspicious and she'd be certain to tell her son of their visit.

"What now?" asked Ryan.

"I'll drop you at Meadowbank Farm and then head home. I've menus and orders to do for the cafe, but I'll see you bright and early at the station in the morning."

"And Jason Williams?"

"We'll see what the inspector has to say."

CHAPTER THIRTY-FIVE

"Well done, that's the first real lead we've had in this case," said Inspector Evans at his briefing the following morning in their team room at Cirencester Police Station.

He leaned against the doorjamb of his office while Keya, Ryan, and Inspector Sue all sat behind their desks. Stan Rowbottom stood against the far wall, facing the inspector.

"I know Jason Williams," remarked Stan.

"Always getting himself into fights in the town centre. But then his mum found him a job with an aggregates company, and he now works all over the country laying roads, car parks and that sort of thing. Come to think of it, he hasn't been in trouble for a while. But this sounds a bit … complex for him."

"He's the only lead we have at the moment, Stan, so you two," Inspector Evans looked from Keya to Ryan, "go and visit him after we've finished our briefing."

"Yes, sir," Ryan and Keya chorused.

The inspector continued, "Constable Jenkins, what can you tell us about the search for the money Mrs Bartlett sent electronically?"

"I've spoken briefly to the team at headquarters. They did follow it for one more step, but then the money was split and sent to different places. They're not confident they'll find it."

"Then we'll be solving this case the old-fashioned way, using our heads and our feet. Let's go over your visit to Cirencester yesterday."

Keya and Ryan explained about their visit to the Moo milkshake bar.

"So at least we have a vague description of the kidnapper. Female, and hiding her head with a hijab."

"Which is interesting," mused Inspector Sue. "As she knew how to wear one so it looked authentic. She didn't just wrap any old headscarf around her head."

"Point taken," accepted Inspector Evans.

"And our witness in the antique centre," began Ryan, "said she was slim, had no discernible accent, and was of average height."

"And she was young, probably in her twenties or early thirties, and spoke politely and quietly," Keya said.

Ryan remembered, "Oh, and she has a pair of violet Converse trainers."

"That's quite a lot," agreed Inspector Evans, "but not enough to give us her address."

There was silence for a minute or so.

Then Keya said, "I don't think she was working alone."

"Why not?" asked Inspector Evans.

"Well, how likely is a young woman to kidnap a toddler for ransom money?"

Inspector Sue spoke up. "Actually, it is common for females of childbearing age, who are pregnant or have lost a child, to abduct a baby. But less likely a toddler, unless the woman lived locally and had seen him in the neighbourhood. But I agree, they would want to keep him, not exchange him for money."

Inspector Evans concluded, "It is conceivable, then, that this woman took the boy, and her husband, boyfriend, or partner, realised what she'd done and took advantage of the situation."

Ryan tapped his keyboard and then said, "Except that the first email we received from the kidnapper we believe she was associated with was at 1 pm."

"And Biljana finally admitted that Zaad disappeared at twenty past eleven," added Inspector Sue.

Keya looked at her colleagues, "Which didn't give a spur-of-the-moment kidnapper much time, and certainly not enough to devise a complex plan involving Rebellion and electronic transfers. The balloon man was spontaneous with his plan, which is why he asked for cash."

"So you think this was premeditated?" queried Inspector Sue.

"Yes, I do," Keya confirmed.

"It's an inside job," Inspector Evans said. "I've always believed so."

"But how can it be?" asked Inspector Sue. "The family were all accounted for, even Nadia."

"Yes, she was staying in Bath with the Bartletts' window cleaner," confirmed Stan, grinning. "I spoke to the manager yesterday."

"But the kidnapper had to know the boy would be in the park on Saturday morning," Inspector Evans argued.

"Except," Keya hesitated, "they could have been waiting and watching for the right time. And Biljana often took the boy to the park."

"That park? And on a Saturday?" queried Ryan.

"That's true. Biljana admitted that she often used a playground closer to Cedar Lane, and the whole family visited my cafe the previous Saturday. So a trip to The Walnut Tree Playing Field was not a regular Saturday morning activity," Keya conceded.

"An inside job," Inspector Evans repeated. "Who would you look to of the family members, Sue?"

They all waited as Inspector Sue scribbled on her notepad.

Then she looked up and said, "I'd start with Biljana, the nanny. It's one thing to be upset, but she was … terrified. I thought it was because she was worried about losing her job, but what if it was something else?

"She'd be an easy target for a would-be kidnapper. Either with an offer of money or a threat to her or her family back home. I've no idea about her past. Apart from Nadia, she was the person I interacted with least in the house, and she locked herself in her room for most of the time Zaad was missing."

"I agree," Inspector Evans declared. "Sergeant Varma and Constable Jenkins. You're following up Jason Williams and the balloon man side of this. Sue, are you visiting the family today?"

"I wasn't going to."

"I think you should. In particular, speak to the nanny. Also, see if you can get anything out of the boy today."

"Can I help?" asked Stan.

"Yes." Inspector Evans looked across at him.

"Reach out to your contacts and see who else employs Bulgarian girls. See if there's somewhere all the girls meet up. Also, if there are any rumours about a network or something which an unscrupulous person might have used to involve the nanny in the kidnapping of Zaad Bartlett."

CHAPTER THIRTY-SIX

Keya, who was wearing her uniform today, collected her official police Ford Focus from the rear station car park.

Originally used by the Traffic Division, it was covered with distinctive blue and yellow checks and had a strip of blue and white lights across its roof.

Pulling the seat forward, she commented to Ryan, "I wonder who's been using my car."

The Ford Focus was much speedier than her Polo, and she had to remind herself to ease off the accelerator when the speedometer swung above the forty miles an hour speed limit as they drove out of Cirencester.

Returning to Fairford, they drove along Moor Lane towards Mrs Williams' house.

Small children, riding their bikes or playing in their front drives, shouted and pointed at the police car while adults stopped and stared.

Keya pulled to a stop in front of Mrs Williams' house. She noted that there were no vehicles parked in the drive.

Once again, they waited for Mrs Williams to open the front door, but at least this time she'd remembered to put her teeth in.

"You won't get Jason today," she said with a smile of satisfaction. "He's working near Yeovil. Come back tomorrow."

"And where will he be working then?"

"How should I know?"

"Mrs Williams, we will speak to your son. We can do so quietly here, or publicly at his work. Here is my number." Keya handed the elderly woman her business card. "I suggest he call me. Today."

"He hasn't done anything wrong," shouted Mrs Williams at their retreating backs.

Keya stopped halfway down the drive, turned round, and replied in a level tone, "Then we won't need to speak to him for very long."

"What now?" asked Ryan when they climbed back into the police car.

"How can we help with the investigation into Biljana?" Keya responded.

"Inspector Sue is speaking to her directly, but what about her friends at the park?"

"Good idea. Let's see if we can find them."

Keya drove round to the side entrance to The Walnut Tree Playing Field and parked beside the stone wall which surrounded it. As they crossed the sports pitches, a group of youths were playing football close to one of the goal posts.

"Are those the kids we met yesterday?" asked Ryan, pointing towards an area where discarded bicycles lay on the ground.

They heard a boy shout, "It's the filth."

"Yes, that's them," Keya confirmed, ignoring other shouts as they walked past the tennis courts. Two out of three were occupied by families knocking tennis balls to each other.

"Out," someone shouted.

The play area was at the farthest end of the playing fields. Another group of teenage boys and girls were sitting on the outdoor exercise equipment, talking rather than actually using it.

But plenty of younger children were enjoying the swings, slides, and climbing frames. Their minders were standing in groups watching, while others were sitting at the metal tables outside the temporary coffee concession trailer.

Inside a green-railed enclosure, several toddlers were scrambling across the climbing frame or were being pushed on the roundabout.

Overall, it was an idyllic scene, and it was hard to imagine that a small boy had been snatched from the area only a few days before.

"Tea?" asked Ryan.

"Oh, yes, please." She smiled up at him. "Thank you."

He smiled back. "I thought it would help us blend in." Which was difficult considering their uniform. "And people might think we're only here for community policing reasons, rather than specifically for the Bartletts case."

At the concession trailer, Ryan ordered their drinks.

"It's a bit late, isn't it? Patrolling here after that boy was snatched," commented the man who took Ryan's order.

"Just making sure it doesn't happen again," replied Ryan politely. "At least the boy is safely back with his parents."

"Do many nannies bring kids to the park?" asked Keya.

"At this time of year it's grandparents, friends, even older school children babysitting younger kids. There's too much pressure on mums to work and earn a living for them to spend the whole summer holidays with their children. It's a shame, really."

He placed their drinks on the counter and said, "Milk and sugar are on the table over there."

"What about the Bulgarian nannies? Do they stick together?"

"I don't know. I only started working this pitch last week. But there are a couple of foreign-speaking girls over there." He pointed towards two women pushing children on the type of swings which had seats especially for younger children.

"Thanks," Keya said, and after pouring milk into her tea, she and Ryan approached the women.

"Hi," she began conversationally.

"You found Zaad," said a young woman with black hair. "Is he OK?"

"He's fine," confirmed Keya. "You know him and Biljana?"

"Oh yes, we meet in park. One or two times a week."

"It must be hard for you being so far away from home."

"Not really," said the blonde-haired woman as she gently pushed the swing. "I like it here. I want to stay."

"And Biljana. Has she made friends here?"

The two women looked at each other and smiled.

"What is it?" asked Keya. Then it dawned on her. "Of course. Her boyfriend."

"Jason is very good to her."

Ryan started. "Not Jason Williams?"

"That's right. He strong and like Bulgarian men, he has tattoos."

"And a shaven head," cried Keya. She turned to Ryan and asked, "What colour football shirts do Aston Villa supporters wear?"

Ryan stared at her. "Maroon. With light blue sleeves."

"Then Jason Williams IS Biljana's boyfriend. Come on. We need to get to Cedar Lane before Inspector Sue leaves."

CHAPTER THIRTY-SEVEN

Keya strode quickly back to her car across the playing fields. Ryan easily kept pace with her, and they both ignored the jeers and taunts of the football playing youths.

Jumping into her car, Keya performed a neat, three-point turn in the lane and drove back to Cedar Lane.

Inspector Sue was standing at the front door speaking to Malika and she gave them a quizzical look when they parked in the drive.

When they climbed out of the police car and approached her, she asked in a cautious voice, "Is everything all right?"

Keya forced herself to smile casually. "Yes, but we need to interview Biljana, and we wondered if you could join us?"

"Why do you want to speak to her?" Malika asked, sounding puzzled.

"Just part of our enquiries as we tie up loose ends," Keya reassured her.

Inspector Sue wore a shrewd expression. She knew there was more to their visit than tying up loose ends. "Would you mind if I come back inside, and my colleagues and I have a chat with Biljana?"

"I suppose not," sighed Malika as she led them into the kitchen. "Use the living room. I've cleaned up after your colleagues."

Keya and Ryan entered the room behind the kitchen, which now smelt of furniture spray. The three-seater sofa, armchairs, and coffee table had been returned to their original positions.

Inspector Sue entered, accompanied by a scared-looking Biljana. They both sat down on the sofa.

Keya decided that there was no point delaying the interview and as the girl looked about to flee, or burst into tears, she asked directly, "Is your boyfriend Jason Williams?"

Biljana leaned forward enquiringly. "Is Jason all right?"

"As far as we know, he's fine," Keya confirmed. "His mum said he's working away today."

"Yes, he works in lots of different places."

"And you usually see him at weekends?"

"Yes." Biljana's voice was hesitant.

"But not this weekend?"

"How could I? With Zaad missing."

"What about Saturday morning? Did he join you in the park?"

"No." Biljana slowly shook her head.

"So you didn't speak to him."

"Only after ..." Biljana clammed up.

"Only after you couldn't find Zaad?"

"Yes," Biljana replied, gulping back tears. "I didn't know what to do."

Inspector Sue placed a hand on Biljana's arm. "You must have been very scared. Did speaking to Jason help?"

Biljana looked at Inspector Sue and nodded. "He told me to call the police."

"Which was the right thing to do."

"So I'm not in trouble?" implored Biljana.

Keya looked across at Inspector Sue, who gave her a subtle shake of the head.

"No, you're not in trouble. Did you see Jason again, say, at church on Sunday morning?"

Biljana smiled and replied, "I first met him at church in May. He usually takes his mum to the Sunday morning services. And this week, he helped her to see the flowers the children had arranged. He only had time to ask me quickly how I was."

"Standing beside the pew?" Keya asked casually.

Biljana tilted her head. Was she trying to work out the meaning behind Keya's question?

Eventually she said a hesitant, "Yes."

"And have you seen him since then?"

"No. He was at football match last night, and he's working today. But I'll see him again at weekend. He's taking me somewhere very exciting. Weston-Super-Mare."

"That'll be lovely," said Sue, before glancing across at Keya.

"Yes, if the weather holds. Thank you for speaking to us."

"Is that it? Can I go?"

"Yes, you can go," Inspector Sue confirmed.

When Biljana had left the room, Inspector Sue said firmly and quietly, "Not now. Discuss it back at the station."

CHAPTER THIRTY-EIGHT

Back at Cirencester Police Station, Keya and Ryan found Stan speaking to Inspector Evans.

Stan said, "And that's all I can tell you. They seem nice girls and are genuinely trying to earn a living and have a better life. And of course, most of them hope to fall in love and marry an Englishman who can look after them for the rest of their lives."

"The modern-day fairy tale," mused the inspector. He looked across at Keya and Ryan and said, "You weren't long. Is Jason Williams a dead end?"

"No, sir. But I think it best we wait for Inspector Sue to discuss our morning's findings."

The inspector hesitated before giving a curt nod of his head. "All right, but someone should put the kettle on."

"I'll do that," volunteered Stan, and he left the team room.

Inspector Evans returned to his office, leaving the door open, and Ryan sat down behind his computer.

Keya also sat down at her desk and checked the messages on her phone. She'd received one earlier from Zivah.

Everything OK here. Busy already. Will we see you later?

Keya replied.

Still in the middle of the case. Yes, I'll try to come in later.

"You beat me back," Inspector Sue said as she walked into the team room, loosening her cream scarf with blue and yellow owls on it.

Her face was slightly flushed. "But then that police car of yours is rather speedy. The chief inspector borrowed it last week, and he gave me a lift."

So that had solved the mystery of who'd used her work car, and the chief inspector was probably not the only one.

Stan returned with a tray of hot drinks and a Tupperware container of homemade biscuits.

"Lemon," approved Keya after she'd snapped off and tried part of a biscuit.

"My wife made them," Stan explained. "She likes to cook, but now the children have left home and married …"

"Right, are we all here?" asked Inspector Evans, stepping out of his office and taking the mug of coffee Stan held out for him. "I take it you made some progress this morning?"

Keya and Ryan looked to Inspector Sue as the senior officer to take the lead.

"I did see little Zaad, but all I could get out of him was the word 'Gami'."

"He was saying that when we found him yesterday," Keya acknowledged. "I think it's his name for his toy rabbit. Mr Flopsy's probably too much for a two-year-old."

"Oh. That would make sense but …"

Inspector Evans leaned forward and asked, "But you think it refers to something else?"

"Something, or someone, but I couldn't work out who. But perhaps Keya is right, and he was just referring to his teddy. And that was all I got from him before Malika whisked him away to play with the nanny." Inspector Sue stopped and looked across at Keya.

"The nanny, yes. Ryan and I called on Jason Williams, but he was out at work. His mum was very uncooperative, but I made it very clear that we needed to speak to him and that it was better he got in touch with us. But we might have to traipse over to Yeovil, or wherever he's working tomorrow."

"Go round again later. But what has this to do with the nanny?"

Keya explained about their trip to The Walnut Tree Playing Field.

"So we returned to Cedar Lane and interviewed Biljana, with Inspector Sue present. And it turns out Biljana's boyfriend is Jason Williams, which I should have realised earlier."

"Why?" asked Inspector Sue.

"Because I saw him collect her from my cafe. Tattoos, shaved head, and all. But I hadn't connected the football shirt he was wearing with his favourite team, until Ryan told me what the colours were."

"Aston Villa play in maroon with blue sleeves," Ryan confirmed.

"So Jason Williams is involved?" queried Inspector Evans, steering the discussion back to the investigation.

Keya sat up as she said, "Biljana called Jason when she realised Zaad was missing. He was the one who told her to call us."

"So?" queried Stan. "Wasn't that the right thing to do?"

Keya turned to Stan and replied, "Totally. But it means Jason was the first person to know about Zaad's disappearance. Probably around half past eleven."

"It was 11.32 according to the call log on Biljana's phone," confirmed Ryan, reading from his computer screen.

"I still don't follow." Stan rubbed his chin.

"I do," growled Inspector Evans. "That made Jason think. He knew the Bartletts had bought that new house, and Biljana had probably told him about the £48,000 in the savings fund."

"Malika and Jonathan were arguing about buying a new car in front of Biljana at my cafe," Keya confirmed.

"So Jason, presumably being at home, types out a ransom note and finds one of the local kids to deliver it," continued Inspector Evans.

"He probably received updates on the case from Biljana on Saturday. When he knew his note was being taken seriously, all he needed to do was work out a place where he could collect the money. But why St Mary's church?"

"Because he takes his mum to the Sunday service most weeks," Ryan explained.

"Which means it's also likely he knew about the rail of clerical garments hanging in the vestry," Keya added.

Stan shook his head and said despondently, "It all sounds rather complex for the Jason Williams I knew, but he's probably learned a thing or two working in that aggregates company. You know how men like to talk."

"Yes," Inspector Sue agreed. "And he probably heard about that case in Gloucester last year where a bank robber escaped with the customers after borrowing one of the female teller's coats and wearing a blonde wig he'd brought with him. He carried the stolen money out in a wheeled shopping bag."

"I remember that case. But they did catch him," Stan said.

"And we'll apprehend Jason," declared the Inspector.

"What's the betting he hasn't done anything with the money and most of it is still stashed at his mother's home? I believe that gives us reasonable grounds for a search warrant. I'll apply for one now. Good work team."

CHAPTER THIRTY-NINE

Keya and Ryan were alone in the team room. Stan had left after collecting Inspector Sue's empty cup and his box of biscuits, and Inspector Sue had excused herself, saying she had a meeting at headquarters.

Inspector Evans was in his office with the door closed.

Keya had just logged onto her computer when Ryan remarked, "There's one thing I don't understand."

"What's that?" asked Keya, looking at him over the top of her monitor.

"The final communication from the kidnapper was a telephone call, not an email. Why?"

Keya considered the question before replying thoughtfully, "Because it was quicker? And if they were with Zaad, it might have been easier to call than send an email."

"I wonder if the call was traced?" Ryan started tapping his keyboard, and Keya returned to her own computer.

She groaned at all the emails she'd received. And she'd forgotten that she'd promised to attend Coln Akeman's annual village fete on Saturday and judge the children's fancy dress competition.

There was also an email from Inspector Sue. She clicked on it and read Sue's comments. As a courtesy, Inspector Sue had forwarded Molly Vogt's court application to see her children.

That was a difficult one, and Keya felt conflicted. She'd seen how Zaad's parents had acted when he was missing.

They'd been desperate to get him home. So desperate, Malika had offered a huge £200,000 reward, which was probably all of their remaining savings.

And Jonathan had been distraught. And he'd felt guilty.

She hoped both of them had realised that nothing was more important on a Saturday morning than spending time with their son. But it was easy for her to say. She didn't have children. And if she did, how many times would her job come before them?

Inspector Evan's door opened, and he declared, "I've got it. The warrant. Let's visit Mrs Williams."

Keya grabbed her police hat as Ryan finished a phone call saying, "I have to go," and they followed the inspector out of the police station.

Keya drove with Inspector Evans in the passenger seat of her Ford Focus and Ryan sitting sideways in the back. They'd have to call for a squad car if they arrested Jason Williams, as he wouldn't fit into her vehicle.

Ryan rang Mrs Williams' doorbell and the three of them waited outside her front door.

"I hope she's not tipping off that son of hers," Inspector Evans grunted.

"There's still no car in the drive," Ryan observed.

"Hmm. I bet she knows it's us though, and she's keeping us waiting on purpose," growled the inspector.

When Mrs Williams finally opened the door, leaning on her walking stick, she wasn't in the least bit intimidated by the presence of three police officers.

"What do you want now? He's not here," she croaked, staring up at Inspector Evans.

The inspector stared back. "We have a warrant," he stated in a flat tone.

"Why do you want one of those? There's nothing here but my

collection of china ornaments." The elderly woman remained steadfast in the doorway.

"It's not what you have that interests us. It's what your son has stashed away in his rooms," countered the inspector.

"Nothing but football magazines."

"Are you going to let us in, or do I have to ask my constable to lift you out of the way?" asked the inspector, his tone still neutral.

Mrs Williams turned her gaze on Ryan and smiled slyly. "Well," she considered, stepping closer to Ryan.

Inspector Evans moved quickly. So quickly he surprised Keya, but the instant Mrs Williams shifted her position, he was past her and into the house.

"Oi!" she cried, hobbling after him, waving her stick.

Grinning at each other, Ryan and Keya entered the house.

In the kitchen at the back of the house, Inspector Evans turned to Mrs Williams and said, "Why don't you make us both a cup of tea while my colleagues visit your son's room? You can tell me about your weekend, and what you and Jason did. I understand you're a God-fearing woman and a regular churchgoer."

Mrs Williams hesitated and over her head, Inspector Evans nodded at Keya.

"Come on," Keya said to Ryan. "Let's find out where Jason keeps his things."

Aunt Beanie had told her that Jason lived in the extension above the garage, so she added, "Let's try through there."

She'd spotted a door at the side of the house.

In front of her, Ryan tried the door, which wasn't locked, and they stepped out into a large garage.

"Nice set-up," Ryan commented approvingly, surveying the gym equipment arranged in the area closest to the door. Beyond it, there were shelves holding the usual eclectic collection of garage items. Passing a large piece of exercise equipment, they moved to the rear of the garage where they found a work bench. Tools were neatly arranged on the wall behind it and there was more equipment stored on some metal shelving units.

"I'll try that door," Ryan suggested as he walked ahead of Keya.

Again, the door in the garage wall was unlocked and Ryan pulled it open. They ascended a narrow staircase with a brown nylon carpet.

Unlike the neatly laid out garage, the flat was a mess. Washing up was stacked in the sink and on the draining board of the small kitchen, and empty beer cans and takeaway boxes littered the living room.

Keya wasn't certain she wanted to look inside Jason's bedroom.

Pulling on a pair of blue latex gloves, she said, "I'll start in the living room if you tackle the bedroom."

After ten minutes, in which Keya had only unearthed mouldy pizza crusts and a pink satin bra, Ryan called through from the bedroom, "I've found it."

When she walked into Jason's bedroom, ignoring the socks and underpants strewn across the floor, Ryan was proudly holding up a rucksack. He said, "Jason didn't even try to hide the evidence. This is the same rucksack Biljana took to church."

"Have you looked inside it?"

"Yes, there are wads of cash. I haven't counted them, but ..."

"It's a good bet it'll be close to £48,000, minus whatever Jason's spent in the past few days."

"I'd say so," agreed Ryan.

"Anything else of interest in here?"

"Like a computer or printer? No."

"OK, bring the rucksack with you and we'll rejoin the Inspector and Mrs Williams."

Keya kept her gloves on and as they entered the main house and returned to the kitchen, she glanced into the dining room. There was a black printer in one corner, beside a wastepaper basket.

Keya walked in and picked a ball of paper out of the bin. Unwrapping it, she read, 'Put the money in the rucksack. Send the nanny to the 10.30 service at St. Mary's and tell her to sit in the back row. Place the rucksack on the floor. No police.'

Keya didn't think it was the same wording as the letter they'd received with the balloon, probably because it was a rough draft.

Looking down at the other balls of paper in the bin, she decided to take them all with her as evidence. The wastepaper basket had a white liner bag which she loosened and lifted out.

When she turned round, Ryan was watching her.

She handed him the crumpled piece of paper and said, "An earlier version of the second ransom letter?"

Ryan read the letter and nodded his head. "It's not exactly the same wording as the one we received, but close enough."

"What are you doing in there?" Mrs Williams called.

Ryan moved back into the corridor and stepped out of Keya's way as she moved to the entrance to the kitchen, still holding the white bin liner.

"And what's that?" asked the elderly lady, sitting at a small Formica kitchen table.

"Rubbish. Including the drafts of the ransom letter your son sent."

Mrs William's mouth dropped open.

"Anything else?" Inspector Evans asked casually.

"The rucksack, and what looks like most of its contents."

"Very good, Sergeant." Turning back to Mrs Williams, the inspector said, "Thank you for the tea. We'll be on our way now."

"Is that it?" asked Mrs Williams uncertainly, her earlier bravado vanishing.

"For now," the inspector responded.

Outside the house, Inspector Evans pulled out his mobile phone and made a call. "Hello, Arthur."

And after a pause, "Yes, it has been a while. Look, time is important on this one. I don't want our suspect getting wind that we're coming. Can you send two officers to The Lintens housing development on the edge of Yeovil?"

He paused for a moment and listened.

"I think that's the one. Craighall Homes is the developer."

He listened again.

"Yes, but the man we want is working for Alliance Aggregates, building the roads, footpaths and drives."

Another pause, and then, "The name of our suspect? Jason Williams."

CHAPTER FORTY

Back at Cirencester Police Station, Keya was enjoying a pesto pasta salad with sun-dried tomatoes, and Ryan was eating a sausage roll when Inspector Sue returned to the team room.

"That was a total waste of time," she complained.

"Each of the police forces present wanted to continue with their own method of preventing child abduction, and most of them refused to listen to any other ideas. How can we promote a coherent approach without inter-force cooperation?"

She looked at Keya's sandwich and added, "And we weren't even offered lunch."

As Inspector Sue pulled a plastic packet of sandwiches out of her large black leather handbag, she asked, "But have you made any more progress?"

"We have," confirmed Inspector Evans from the doorway to his office.

"And we've been enjoying some inter-force cooperation. Avon and Somerset Police picked Jason Williams up for us after Constable Ryan found the rucksack and ransom money in his apartment at Moor Lane. And Sergeant Varma spotted a printer in his mother's dining room and a draft version of the ransom letters in the bin next to it. It's enough evidence to interview him, and probably to charge him. But we'll see what he has to say for himself when the two officers I sent to collect him return."

Keya continued to munch her salad as she listened to the exchange.

"So that's one ransom payment and culprit found, and one to go," concluded Inspector Sue.

Finishing her mouthful, Keya said, "I still think the young woman Ryan and I kept missing on Monday wasn't working alone."

Inspector Sue perched on her desk and looked from Keya to Inspector Evans. "And if you think that it's an inside job, where does that leave us?"

"You interviewed Biljana. Do you think she knew what Jason was doing, or was she involved in the actual kidnapping? I keep coming back to her as she was with the boy," Inspector Evans said.

"Your thoughts, Sergeant?" Inspector Sue prompted.

"I don't think she had anything to do with Zaad's disappearance," Keya replied. "But what about Jonathan Bartlett? He changed his routine and went to a gallery opening. But have we confirmed he actually went, and do we know how long he was there?"

"No, we don't," admitted Inspector Evans. "And that is a lead you could follow up, Sergeant."

"Jonathan was genuinely upset his son was missing," mused Inspector Sue, "but he does like his toys, and he's dependent on his wife for money. An extra £200,000 would do very nicely, for a while."

"You mean he could have tricked his wife into paying him that money, rather than keep it in their savings?" asked Ryan.

Inspector Sue nodded. "Malika had control of the accounts, and therefore, the money."

Keya considered this statement, before adding, "At my cafe I overheard Jonathan ask his wife for money for a new car. One that was more in keeping with his perceived social status. But Malika appeared very practical and told him they had a perfectly acceptable car. Also, that after buying the new house, which, by the way, she said cost more because Jonathan insisted on having his own studio, they needed to be careful with their spending."

"Which proves Sue's point," Inspector Evans asserted. "The husband is dependent on his wife for money, and he's a social climber.".

"I suppose that's one way of putting it," conceded Inspector Sue.

"Let's look into his background before we speak to him. Constable, can you do that?" Inspector Evans asked Ryan.

"Yes, sir,"

"And Sergeant, you'll check his alibi. Sue, would you like to join me to interview Jason Williams?'

"I'd be delighted."

With their tasks established for the afternoon, Inspector Sue, Ryan, and Keya settled back to eat their lunch.

Stan appeared with another tray of drinks.

"You really shouldn't, Stan," said Sue appreciatively. "It's not your job to be our tea boy."

"I was the tea boy when I started at this police station. And do you know what was so great about it?"

"No?" Inspector Sue said.

"I got to find out what everyone else was doing."

Ryan laughed.

"And I was wondering if there are any updates on your case?"

Keya and Ryan told him and Inspector Sue, about their visit to Mrs Williams.

"Daft lad," Stan remarked. "But not a bad plan. And he didn't actually hurt anyone."

Sue stiffened. "He took advantage of a distressed couple whose child was missing."

"True, but he didn't actually take the boy."

"No," admitted Inspector Sue.

Keya finished her salad and picked up her mobile phone. She called Finn Andrews, her artist friend.

When he answered, she said, "Hi, can you meet me at the cafe in an hour, and are Lady Violet or Jarrod free to come with you?"

"Is this about my paintings, or something else?"

"We have sold a painting, but it's about something else. A police matter."

"Jarrod's here, and he's been meaning to visit your cafe. I'll persuade him to come with me."

"See you soon."

Keya finished the call as Ryan said, "Stan, if you're not busy this afternoon, could you help me with some research into Jonathan Bartlett?"

"The father of the kidnapped child? Interesting. Of course I'll help."

Keya pushed back her chair and said, "And I'm going to check out his alibi."

Keya changed out of her uniform before leaving the station and drove to the Waterwheel Cafe in her Polo.

As she entered the antique centre, Gilly looked up and waved. She finished speaking to a tall gentleman and made her way across to Keya, intercepting her before she reached the first row of stalls.

"How is Zaad?" asked Gilly in a quiet voice.

"I didn't see him when I was at his house this morning, and even Inspector Sue's had very little time with him. His mother is keeping him close to her."

"Good thing too, after what happened. What a relief he's back home. Now, I wanted to catch you to discuss this weekend. The Women's Institute has decided they don't want to serve drinks and cakes to the general public. They'll still provide lunch to those who buy a ticket in advance, and, of course, they'll be running a stall selling their jams, bakes, and homegrown produce."

Keya listened with a flutter of apprehension in her stomach.

Gilly continued, "So I know it's late notice, but it would be great advertising for the cafe if you could run a stall there."

"But I'm supposed to be judging the children's fancy dress."

"I can find someone else for that. Don't worry."

"Has a coffee vendor been booked?" Keya asked.

"Yes. The Coffee Bean are taking a pitch," Gilly confirmed.

"So there isn't much point in us serving hot drinks as well, especially as we can't easily move our coffee machine and it will still be needed here, at the cafe."

Gilly frowned. "I see what you mean."

"Look, I've a meeting at the cafe soon, and I should check in with Zivah beforehand, so why don't we sit down later and decide what's best to do?"

Gilly placed her hand on Keya's arm, and, in a relieved voice, she said, "Great idea. And I'll find the list of stalls which have already confirmed."

Keya passed through the antique centre, returning the greetings of several stallholders, before entering the cafe. It was half past two, so the lunchtime crowd was dispersing and, for most customers, it was too early for afternoon tea.

"Trust you to arrive after all the hard work's been done," grinned Zivah as Keya entered. She lowered her voice and said, "And we had another reporter in from the Cirencester Times."

Keya tilted her head and enquired, "An older man, with sallow skin and sunken eyes."

"That's the one. Ronnie Marsh. And he saw the quiche Monica brought in for us to try and asked for a piece."

"I bet he didn't pay for it," Keya scoffed.

Zivah's face tightened as she enquired, "Wasn't he a reporter? Shouldn't I have given him a free meal?"

Keya sighed. "He is a reporter, but a rather unscrupulous one. I doubt he'll actually write anything about the cafe, but you did well. It's worthwhile keeping him onside, otherwise he could be trouble."

Zivah smiled in relief.

"He did enjoy the quiche. In fact, he said it was delicious." Zivah hesitated before adding, "And he said the same about the piece of Aunt Beanie's lemon drizzle cake he ate."

"I'm sure both Monica and Aunt Beanie will be delighted he enjoyed their baking. But watch out for him coming in again. I don't want to be feeding him for free on a regular basis."

"OK," Zivah replied, with less than her usual enthusiasm.

Keya took a deep breath. Attempting to sound positive and upbeat, she said, "And you never know, he might give us a glowing report in this week's paper. And what else has been happening?"

"We were so busy at lunchtime that both Monica and Aunt Beanie helped out. Amma confided that she prefers Monica in the kitchen, but Aunt Beanie did a great job with the sandwiches, even if she was a little too enthusiastic with the fillings. But it meant Thomas was free to serve customers. The older ladies do love him. He's even getting tips which he offered to share with us, but I told him to keep them. I hope that's OK?"

"It's a great idea. Where is Thomas now?"

"He'd done his hours for today, so Aunt Beanie took him home. I told him to come later tomorrow, and cover the lunch and afternoon teas." Zivah hesitated before suggesting, "It's great having extra help, but I think we ought to formalise it."

"You mean actually employ Aunt Beanie?"

"And Monica. She was so excited to be here. I know she'd love to help."

"Let's think about it. But I have a meeting now about the kidnapping case."

"I thought you'd found the boy?"

"We have, but there's still the question of who took him and where the money went."

CHAPTER FORTY-ONE

Despite it being summer, and warm and clammy outside, the grey-haired Jarrod Willcox walked confidently into the cafe wearing a pair of red corduroy trousers, with a matching bow tie, and long-sleeved blue shirt.

He was accompanied by Finn Andrews, looking presentable in a pair of light-blue chinos and a teal-green polo shirt.

"This is marvellous," greeted Jarrod as he strode across and hugged Keya. Letting go, he glanced over her shoulder and declared, "And who is this? Your sister?"

"Hi, I'm Zivah."

Zivah held out her hand and Jarrod took it. He also took hold of her left hand and admired her rings. "And recently married. Congratulations."

Zivah blushed. "Thank you. Can I get you something to drink, and perhaps a slice of cake?"

"Wonderful. A latte for me, and you choose the cake. Finn?"

"A cappuccino please, and a piece of chocolate cake," replied Finn. "And I hear you sold one of my paintings?"

"Oh, you're the artist," enthused Zivah. "Yes, we sold the one of three trees." Zivah looked down at the oversize black canvas case Finn was carrying and asked, "Is that a replacement?"

"Another three paintings, actually, if you're happy to have them?"

Keya said, "Zivah, why don't you and Finn discuss where to hang the paintings, and I'll sit outside with Jarrod? I think the sun's trying to come out."

Keya led Jarrod outside, and they sat at a table on the edge of the patio, closest to the river, and away from other customers.

Jarrod said, "Finn told me you wanted to discuss a police matter. Is it another fake painting?" Keya had visited Jarrod in the past to ask him to confirm whether a painting was genuine or not.

"No, I'm checking the alibi of a potential suspect, but it's rather delicate."

"Go on," Jarrod encouraged her.

At that moment, one of the students placed a round black tray on their table, removing their drinks and two pieces of almond slice from it.

"Thank you," Keya said, before the student lifted her tray and moved away.

Keya turned back to Jarrod and said, "The father of the boy that went missing, Jonathan Bartlett..."

Jarrod wrinkled his nose in distaste.

"...said he was at one of your exhibition openings on Saturday," Keya finished.

"He was," Jarrod confirmed, "although I've no idea how he got his hands on an invitation. It was a private viewing with a specially curated guest list."

"How long did he stay?"

"Until we had to kick him out, so between half past twelve and a quarter to one."

Keya sat back and picked up her cup of tea.

"That wasn't what you wanted to hear, was it?"

"Not really."

"He's a braggart," proclaimed Jarrod distastefully. "He loves to put down other artists, and pontificate over paintings. And I'll give him his due. He does look the part, but his work ..."

Jarrod wore a pained expression as he shook his head before continuing, "If he allowed himself to be authentic, he might actually be able to paint. But he produces works based on this theme, or that school, and they are, quite frankly, no good. I've refused to display his paintings in our exhibitions several times."

Keya sipped her tea before commenting, "So he's unlikely to make a living from his painting."

Jarrod bit into his almond slice and, as Keya waited for him to answer, she also tried the traybake. It had a thin, crisp pastry base, a layer of raspberry jam, and a topping of dense almond sponge. And it was delicious.

"Excellent," Jarrod announced.

"At the moment, Jonathan Bartlett can't persuade anyone to hold an exhibition of his paintings and there is no chance he can make a living from them. But I think he enjoys that. The starving artist persona. But I bet if he no longer had his wife's financial support, we'd see a different side to him.

"Although, as I said, I've refused to buy or exhibit any of his paintings, I once saw a portrait he'd drawn in art school, and it was excellent. If he wanted to, he could make a living as a portrait artist, or even more viable these days, take commissions to draw people's pets."

Keya frowned. "It sounds a bit beneath him."

"Exactly, which is why he spends his time at other people's exhibitions, like the one on Saturday, talking loudly and pompously about the paintings while being supported by his hard-working wife."

"Do you think he's clever?" Keya asked, thinking that even though Jonathan was at the exhibition, his female accomplice could still have snatched Zaad.

"Goodness, no. He's all bravado, and that's the problem. He doesn't actually think."

"So you don't think he'd be able to put together a complex plan?"

"I doubt it."

Keya stared down at the river. Jonathan could still have been involved, and the woman could have been the brains behind the kidnapping and ransom demand. But what did Jonathan have to gain?

£200,000 was a lot of money. But Malika probably earned that amount, or close to it, in a month and, from what Jarrod was saying, Jonathan was on to a good thing. He could continue actually doing very little, pretending to paint, and spending time with his son and the yummy mummies.

Jarrod leaned forward and asked, "Has this conversation helped?"

"I think so. You see, and I shouldn't tell you this, but I know you've kept secrets in the past. We think someone within the Bartletts' household was behind the kidnapping."

"I wondered if that was the case," Jarrod said shrewdly. "I presume the first person you looked into was the nanny?"

"Yes, and she, well, let's say she had nothing to do with the boy's disappearance."

"So next you're looking at the father, as he is an out-of-work artist with a taste for the finer things in life."

"Exactly."

"So who does that leave? Mrs Bartlett and her sisters. Of whom one was staying with her, I saw from the news." Jarrod smiled indulgently and Keya presumed he was referring to Nadia's weekend away with the window cleaner.

"Yes, Nadia enjoyed the attention of the cameras. But hold on. You said sisters. Is there more than one?"

"Yes, Jonathan once showed me a painting - it was dreadful - of his wife and her two sisters. Mrs Bartlett is the middle one."

"We're only aware of Nadia, the older one."

"I can see that's got you thinking. And here's something else I noticed from the news coverage. How did the kidnapper know to take the child's favourite toy?"

"Because he had it with him when he was taken?"

"In the playground? I don't know much about toddlers, but they are somewhat unsteady and use their hands as much as their feet when climbing on things."

"That's a good point. If he wasn't holding his rabbit, how did the kidnapper know to take that particular toy?"

CHAPTER FORTY-TWO

Finn and Zivah joined Keya and Jarrod on the patio outside the Waterwheel Cafe.

Zivah stood beside the table and said, "We've replaced the purchased painting and hung up the other two."

"And customers are already interested in them," Finn smiled.

"Very good, and now we must be getting back." Jarrod finished his coffee and placed his cup back on its saucer.

"I promised we'd take a stall at Coln Akeman's fete on Saturday, and I need to work out what stock to display. Cards always sell well at such events. They're a low-ticket item and they're good for us as they advertise the business. But I need to consider which pictures to use, and to obtain permission from the artists. You should choose one of your paintings, Finn."

Finn's smile widened.

"I think we're also taking a stall at the fete, so I'll see you there," Keya said, pushing her chair back.

"And let's hope you've cleared up the business we discussed by then." Jarrod stood up and he and Finn walked away from the cafe, towards the back of the auction house, from which they'd take a track back to the car park.

Keya was watching them leave when she heard Gilly call, "There you are. Is now a good time to sit down and discuss the fete?"

Keya turned to face Gilly, who was moving towards her, and said, "It is, but I have one phone call to make first." She left Gilly talking to Zivah and walked down the steps to the riverbank. Taking her phone out of her pocket, she phoned Ryan.

"Have you confirmed Jonathan Bartlett's alibi?" he asked.

"I have. He was at the gallery exhibition, just as he said he was. Jarrod Willcox knows him and said that his paintings aren't very good, although if he put his mind to it, he could be a decent portrait artist."

"That tallies with what I've found out. He got by at school and showed promise at art college. He and some other students got into trouble at Henley Regatta one year, but it wasn't anything serious. He then held various jobs at art galleries until he married Malika. Since their marriage, he hasn't worked in the sense of being employed."

"You mean he puts his profession down as artist?"

"That's right. And he's completed tax returns as such for the past five years, but hasn't made a profit."

Which fitted with the information Jarrod had given her.

Keya said, "Which all adds up him to him relying on his wife's salary to pay the bills."

"Yes, and the extras he likes," added Ryan. "He's a member of the exclusive Soho Farmhouse Club with a monthly membership of £166. And I've found plenty of payments to restaurants all over the Cotswolds where he's lunched."

"So any indications he has had, or is having an affair?" Keya wondered if that could be a motive for needing the £200,000. To pay a blackmailer, or debts or expenses he didn't want his wife knowing about.

"I wondered about that too, but despite all his cosy lunches with the yummy mummies, there's not even a whisper about an affair. I did find one comment saying that he might be gay."

"Thanks, Ryan. Let's see what else turns up. And if you and Stan have time, can you also look into Malika's sister for me? Not Nadia, a younger one."

"Called?"

"I've no idea of her name. Jarrod Willcox mentioned her to me. I find it strange none of the family mentioned her before."

"Maybe they're estranged."

"Perhaps. I'm still at the cafe, so I'll probably go straight home after my meeting with Gilly. And she's waiting for me, so unless there's anything else."

There wasn't, so Keya finished her call and returned to the table on the patio, where Gilly was sitting alone, consulting a thin, plastic bound folder.

"Sorry about that," Keya apologised. "I needed to catch up with Ryan and ask him to look into something for me."

"Still working on the kidnapping case?"

"Yes, and it's very frustrating. I don't feel we're making any progress, although ..."

"Yes?" Gilly said, looking innocently eager.

"I better not say anything just yet. So what about the fete?" Keya asked.

Looking slightly disappointed, Gilly explained, "The Women's Institute is providing their sit-down lunch as we discussed. All judges and helpers go along to that. The Scouts are running a BBQ and the Brownies a chocolate fountain. And The Axeman pub is running the bar."

"So with the Women's Institute cake stall, I'm not sure that leaves much for us to do?"

"I must admit, I thought that too, so I rang one of the committee members. She suggested you do an all-day afternoon tea. Perhaps with different options and price levels. People could order the full works, or a light-bite version.

"And then maybe a build your own menu, so those who'd just like sandwiches can have them, or they order sandwiches and a cake, but no tea. Do you see what I mean?"

"I do, but it sounds complicated. And I don't know what staff I'll have as we'll still be running the cafe here, which is getting busier and more popular."

"That's a good thing, isn't it?" Gilly sounded confused.

"Of course. But we're not set up to be full all the time, and with this case ..."

Gilly placed a hand on Keya's arm. "Just do the best you can. And if you don't want to make food to order, why not prepare a buffet for people to choose so many pieces for a certain price?"

"That might work," Keya agreed. "What are Thomas and Oliva doing for the fete?"

"Thomas would love to come, but we've told him he has a job now and if you want him at the cafe, that's where he has to be. And Oliva is helping run the raffle, which she loves doing."

"Great, Thomas can help at the fete. I could ask Aunt Beanie, but she probably has a job already."

"She usually helps the Horticultural Society run their plant stall, but I'm sure she could help you set up."

"OK, we'll do something," agreed Keya. "I just need to think what."

"That's fabulous." Gilly grinned.

"And I haven't asked what you'll be doing."

"Oh, I organise a tent with some of the other stallholders from the antique centre. We mostly sell bric-a-brac, which people love browsing. The fete's actually a large event for a small village, and usually attracts a good crowd."

Keya had only been expecting those in the village to attend. If it was popular with other people in the area, then the fete would be a good place for her to advertise the cafe.

She really needed to spend some quality time working out what to offer on her stall.

Her phone buzzed.

"I'll let you take that." Gilly rose to her feet as Keya answered the call from Ryan.

"I thought I ought to let you know. Malika Bartlett does have a younger sister. And she fits the description of the woman wearing the hijab. Young, slim, and average height. I even found a photo on Instagram of her wearing a pair of pink or pale purple converse trainers."

"Good work, Ryan. And what's her name?"

"Gamira Jabara."

Keya smiled and said, "Gami."

CHAPTER FORTY-THREE

"What do you mean, Gami?" asked Ryan on the other end of Keya's phone call.

"That's the word Zaad kept using after we found him. I thought he was referring to his toy rabbit," Keya explained. She was still sitting on a chair on the patio of her cafe, looking out across the River Coln.

"Of course, Inspector Sue said she heard him use it too. Do you think that's because he was asking for his aunt, or telling us he'd been with her?"

"It could be either. But that word, the description of her appearance, and the fact she'd have known which was Zaad's favourite toy, do make her our prime suspect, don't you think?"

Ryan sounded excited as he added, "And that would explain why Zaad went with her without creating a fuss. His favourite aunt."

"Especially if she already had his rabbit, and perhaps an ice cream."

Ryan said seriously, "But why would she want to kidnap her little nephew?"

"Does she have financial problems?"

"I'll need to look into it."

Keya sighed. "I better come back to the station."

The team room was full when Keya returned to Cirencester Police Station in the late afternoon.

Stan was standing beside Ryan's desk, and they were both listening to Inspector Evans, who was standing in the doorway to his office. Inspector Sue was leaning against Keya's desk.

"Of course, he denied having anything to do with the kidnapping," explained Inspector Evans.

"As technically, he didn't," Stan observed.

Inspector Sue frowned and said, "He also denied knowing anything about a balloon and ransom notes for £48,000, until Dai held up the rucksack you found, Constable, and started removing wads of cash from it."

"Which he tried to fob off as football winnings," added Inspector Evans.

"But the draft letters Sergeant Varma found were the key." Inspector Sue looked across at Keya, who was hovering in the doorway.

"After we produced several of those, Jason Williams groaned in acceptance and started telling us a sob story about how he wanted the money for his elderly mother, and the Bartletts didn't really need it as Jonathan only wanted to use it to buy a flashy new car."

"So we were right," said Keya, entering the room and standing beside Inspector Sue's desk. "Biljana told him about the conversation at my cafe, and perhaps others she'd overheard."

"Jason admitted that's why he asked for that particular sum."

"I can't say I blame him," Stan defended Jason. "I heard his mum's been on the hospital waiting list for a new knee for over a year. With that money, he could have paid for a private operation."

"It was still wrong. And he has been charged," Inspector Evans informed them.

"What sentence will he get?" Keya asked.

"The maximum for extortion or blackmail is fourteen years," stated Inspector Evans.

Stan winced.

"But this was a one-off offence, no violence was used or threatened, and no criminal damage was done ..."

"And he'll plead that he's his mum's carer," Inspector Sue interrupted.

"So I think he'll probably get away with a suspended sentence, and a considerable number of community service hours," Inspector Evans concluded.

"Then he shouldn't lose his job." Stan sounded relieved.

"Probably not." Inspector Evans drew in a deep breath and looked round the room.

His gaze focused on Keya as he enquired, "I thought you were going home from the café?"

"I was, sir, but we've had a breakthrough in the actual kidnapping case. Ryan, I mean Constable Jenkins, what have you discovered?"

"Excuse me," Inspector Sue said, squeezing past Keya to sit behind her desk.

Keya also used the opportunity to sit down on her office chair.

Ryan finished tapping his keyboard and looked up. He began, "Sergeant Varma asked me to look for a second sister."

"What second sister?" asked Inspector Evans. "Does Jonathan Bartlett have a sister?"

"I'm not sure, but it's his wife's younger sister I've been looking into."

Inspector Evans held his hands up. "Let's backtrack. You, Stan, and Sergeant Varma were looking into Jonathan Bartlett. What did you find out?"

Ryan looked at Keya, who recounted her discussion with Jarrod Willcox.

When she finished, Ryan added, "And that correlated with what we found out, didn't it, Stan?" Ryan looked up at the older man, who nodded.

"So you don't think Jonathan Bartlett was behind the kidnapping?"

"Probably not," considered Keya. "But if he was, someone else probably devised the plan."

"Which led you to look at Mrs Bartlett's sisters?" Inspector Evans enquired.

Keya nodded. "It was something Jarrod said, so I asked Constable Jenkins to look into it."

Inspector Evans turned his gaze back to Ryan.

"Malika Bartlett has two sisters. Nadia, the older one who we've met, and a younger sister who we haven't, called Gamira Jabara."

Inspector Sue sat up.

Keya turned to her and said, "Gami."

"Yes, exactly what I was thinking," admitted Inspector Sue.

"Continue, Constable," Inspector Evans growled.

"It was easy to find out about Gamira, as she's an avid user of social media. And she fits the description of the woman who was at the milkshake bar, and then later in the antique centre. But," Ryan looked across at Keya, "we can't find a reason for her to kidnap her young nephew."

"Did you check her medical records?" asked Inspector Sue.

"We don't have access to them," replied Ryan.

"I can sort that out in the morning." Inspector Sue scribbled a note on a pad on her desk. "As I think I told you, women who've lost children sometimes feel an insatiable urge to replace them. That might be why she took Zaad, especially if he was with his nanny on a Saturday morning, when she thought he should be with his parents."

"But why the money?" enquired Inspector Evans.

The team room was silent.

Eventually Inspector Evans said, "Constable Jenkins?"

"I haven't found any debts, or any reason she needed money. She has a well-paid job in the technical department of a company in Worcester."

"Keep digging, but not tonight," Inspector Evans instructed.

"Well done, team. We've solved half the puzzle and my gut tells me we are getting closer to working out the other half."

A police constable looked into the team room and said nervously, "Inspector?"

"Yes?" Inspector Evans and Inspector Sue both replied.

The policewoman looked at Inspector Evans with wide, frightened eyes, and said, "You've not been answering your phone."

"No, I didn't have it with me while interviewing a suspect."

"It's your mother, sir. She's had a fall, and been taken to Cheltenham Hospital by ambulance."

Inspector Evans paled.

"Go, Dai. We're finished here for the day, and I can cover for you tomorrow if need be," Inspector Sue urged.

Inspector Evans grabbed his phone from his desk before striding out of the team room.

Keya watched him leave and said, "I hope Mrs Evans is OK."

CHAPTER FORTY-FOUR

Keya drove home, worried about Inspector Evans' mum. Ryan had promised to let Aunt Beanie know that she'd been taken into hospital.

Sitting in her small kitchen, which she felt she'd hardly spent any time in recently, Keya twirled a pencil and stared at a pad of paper as she considered what to offer at Coln Akeman's fete on Saturday.

She didn't have much time to prepare, especially when her brain kept returning to Gamira Jabora. Why had Malika's sister kidnapped Zaad?

Gamira must have treated him well, as the boy was uttering her name when they found him at the antique centre. At least his experience was one of a weekend away with a loving relative, rather than being imprisoned by a stranger.

But she returned to the principal question. Why?

Keya shook her head. Perhaps Inspector Sue would find the answer in Gamira's medical records.

Back to her plans for Saturday. Gilly's suggestion of a buffet was a good one, and she should keep it simple. A selection of sandwiches, traybakes, biscuits and small sausage rolls.

Hotels and restaurants charged a lot for afternoon teas, but the fete was more about raising brand awareness for the Waterwheel Cafe, rather than making money.

She could offer a cream tea with a scone, jam, and clotted cream, along with a cup of tea for £5.00. Then a selection of five pieces from the buffet with tea for £10.00, and seven pieces for £12.00.

She'd see what teas they had, but she'd probably serve Earl Grey, Darjeeling, and vanilla chai as a minimum.

The following morning, Keya woke up, her mind still grappling with the idea that Gamira had kidnapped her own nephew.

She quickly showered and dressed and, grabbing a clean white shirt to go with her uniform, she drove straight to the police station.

Nobody was in the team room when she arrived and turned on the lights. She changed into her uniform, made herself a cup of tea, and settled at her desk with the prepared fruit salad and strawberry yoghurt she'd grabbed from her fridge.

Turning on her computer, she checked her emails. There were too many for her to concentrate on at the moment.

She felt restless. But also that she was missing something.

"Morning," Ryan greeted her cheerfully, as he entered the team room carrying a laptop case over his shoulder.

"Mum was really chuffed customers enjoyed her quiche, but then they are really tasty with loads of filling and crisp pastry."

Keya looked up and asked, "Do you know what's she's doing for the rest of this week, and on Saturday?"

"Not much, I don't think. Why? Do you want her to help at the cafe?"

"Actually, Gilly's persuaded me to take a stall at Coln Akeman's fete and, with this case still hanging over us, I'm not sure I'll have enough time to prepare for it. And I can't ask Zivah and Amma as they're so busy with the cafe."

"I'm sure she'd love to help. Let me call her." Ryan sat down at his desk and took his phone out of his pocket.

When his call was answered, he said, "Hi, Mum. Are you busy this week, or could you help Keya prepare for Coln Akeman's fete on Saturday?"

He listened and then looked at Keya and asked, "What do you need?"

"I … shall I speak to her?"

"Just a sec, Mum. I'll pass my phone to Keya."

"Hi, Monica. That was a lovely quiche you brought to the cafe yesterday," said Keya, speaking into Ryan's phone.

"I'm glad you liked it. I wondered if you might want more of them?"

"Quite possibly. But I need to sit down with my mum and Zivah after we've finished this case and work through everything. We've been much busier than we expected to be since we opened."

"Of course. And is the little boy all right?"

"He seems to be, yes. But the reason I asked Ryan to call you is that I've been asked to run a stall selling afternoon teas on Saturday, at Coln Akeman's fete. I was thinking about four or five sandwich fillings, some biscuits and traybakes, and some sausage rolls or mini quiches. Also, scones with homemade jam and clotted cream."

"That's sounds a wonderful idea, and the weather forecast is for sunny weather this Saturday. What would you like me to do?"

"What can you do?"

"All of it! I'll start baking today and then let me know your ideas for the sandwich fillings. Who do you have to help out on Saturday?"

"Me and Thomas, Gilly's son. That's all for the moment."

"I can help, and we can ask Ryan."

Keya looked up at Ryan with a quizzical expression.

"What?" he asked.

"Can you help at our afternoon tea stall on Saturday?"

In her ear she heard Monica say, "But he's not to eat everything."

"As long as you feed me."

Keya smiled. To Monica she said, "Yes, he'll help. But you're right, we'll have to make sure he leaves some food for the customers."

"Oi!" exclaimed Ryan, before removing his laptop from its bag.

"I'll let you go," said Monica. "Ryan can give me your number and before that, I'll update him with my progress."

"Thank you so much." Keya ended the call, and said to Ryan, "I hope that's OK? Helping me out this weekend."

"It sounds fun, and I know Mum will be in her element. Besides, I've never visited that fete. Maybe I'll win a giant teddy bear.

Keya began. "Talking of cuddly toys ..."

"Speaking about me again?" Inspector Evans interrupted as he entered the room.

"Sir. We weren't expecting you this morning. How's your mum?" Keya asked.

"Sore. She was X-rayed last night and is seeing the consultant this morning, but the nurses told me her hip is fractured and they think she'll go in for surgery this afternoon."

"Shouldn't you be with her?"

"I thought I'd check in with you, and leave," he consulted his watch, "at ten for the hospital, unless they contact me earlier."

He removed his phone from his brown suit jacket pocket and held it up. "And the ringer is on loud today."

"Very good, sir."

"You were talking about cuddly toys," Inspector Evans reminded Keya.

"Oh, yes. Only that I was about to ask Ryan what he'd found out, as he took his laptop home with him last night."

"Not much," confessed Ryan. "Gamira has a steady job with a reasonable income, no debts, no questionable boyfriends or friends, and she's loyal to her family."

"To her family," Keya repeated.

"Morning, everyone," said Inspector Sue brightly as she entered the team room wearing a bright yellow and green floral dress. She was carrying her large black handbag and black jacket.

"How's your mother, Dai?" she asked as she hung her jacket up on a peg behind her desk.

"They think she's broken her hip and she'll need surgery this afternoon. But before you say it, I'm just checking in and then I'll go back to the hospital."

"Don't linger too long, and I hope your mum's not in too much pain. Now, I've had a message that Gamira's medical records have been sent over, so I'll check them out."

"I'll be mother," said Inspector Evans, leaving the room.

"He'll be what?" queried Ryan.

"I think he means he'll make the teas and coffees," Inspector Sue explained as she rolled her chair closer to her desk and switched on her computer.

Keya finished her breakfast and, feeling slightly guilty for not separating out the recycled sections, she threw the empty containers into her bin.

"Before I check the medical records, I wanted to update you, Keya, on Molly Vogt's court application. There has been a consultation with her, and her husband in France, and it's been decided that this year she'll have weekly contact with her girls online.

"If all goes well, Didier will be ordered to bring the girls back to the UK at least once to visit their mother in person next year. It's not ideal, but at least it's a step in the right direction. Now, let's look through these records," Inspector Sue said eagerly.

Keya waited, and Ryan had also stopped typing and was looking across at Inspector Sue.

"Here we are." Inspector Evans carried two mugs, and he placed one on Inspector Sue's desk. Ryan looked up expectantly as Inspector Evans sipped from the second mug.

Keya looked down, hiding her grin.

She heard, "Morning. Tea for you, Keya. Let me exchange this for your old cup, and coffee for you, Ryan." Stan had followed Inspector Evans into the room with two more cups.

"Oh," said Inspector Sue flatly.

"Which means?" Inspector Evans enquired.

"There's nothing in Gamira's medical records to explain the kidnapping. No history of mental health issues, or self-harming, and she hadn't been pregnant. In fact, apart from needing contraception, she hasn't visited the doctor in the past eighteen months."

"What does that tell you?" asked Inspector Evans.

Inspector Sue looked up, her eyebrows drawn together in an expression of concern. "That she knew exactly what she was doing, and there was no psychological reason for her taking Zaad."

Keya heard a loud ringing, and Inspector Evans removed his phone from his jacket pocket. Answering it, he listened to the caller before saying, "I'll come now."

He finished the call and looked round at his team, who were all staring at him. "Mother's operation has been brought forward. Keep working on this. I'm certain you're on the right track, and keep me informed."

As he walked past Inspector Sue's desk, she said in a sympathetic tone, "I hope everything goes smoothly."

Inspector Evans left the room muttering, "So do I."

CHAPTER FORTY-FIVE

The team room was silent after Inspector Evans left to be with his mother in hospital.

Inspector Sue leaned back in her office chair and asked, "Sergeant Varma, what were you thinking when I arrived? You were talking about family."

"Was I?"

Ryan offered, "I'd just told you that Gamira has a steady job with a reasonable income, no debts, no questionable boyfriends or friends, and she's loyal to her family."

"Oh, that's right. It was the family loyalty which caught my attention. How loyal?"

"Are you suggesting what I'm thinking?" queried Inspector Sue.

"I'm not sure. What are you thinking?"

"That Malika Bartlett was involved in kidnapping her own son."

There was silence in the room, broken by Stan whistling.

"It seems hard to believe," Keya began.

"But I've seen desperate mothers do far worse," admitted Inspector Sue.

"To protect their children, yes," Keya agreed. "But who was threatening Zaad? There's nothing on file about abuse within the family. Jonathan doesn't seem the violent type, although you never can tell."

"It's the quiet ones you have to watch out for," insisted Stan.

"And Malika is the quieter one in that relationship," commented Inspector Sue.

"My mum cried when I moved to Meadowbank Farm," Ryan said, "even though I'd left home once before, and I'm twenty-three."

Keya's eyes widened. She'd never been certain of Ryan's age.

"Your point is, Ryan?" asked Stan.

"I never saw Malika shed a tear over her missing son."

Inspector Sue looked up, examining the ceiling, and Keya bit her lip. What emotions had Malika shown?

"She was annoyed about the kidnapping," Keya reflected.

"About the ransom demand," Ryan corrected. "She kept asking the chief inspector how he knew the note was genuine, and what other demands had been received."

Keya sat up and exclaimed, "Because she knew there was another one. One she or her younger sister had sent."

"She did hold out for a long time against paying the £48,000," agreed Inspector Sue. "But eventually she paid it."

"Because she didn't have much choice, even though she knew it wasn't going to the kidnapper."

"But then she offered the reward, didn't she?" Stan queried.

"A surprisingly large reward," reflected Inspector Sue.

"We tried to talk her out of it and to offer the usual £50,000, as we were concerned about being inundated with prank calls. But she was insistent, £200,000, and she even persuaded her bank manager to terminate her savings and investments without penalty and transfer all the funds into her current account."

"She was liquidating her assets," Ryan stated.

"Which is something you might do when you're getting divorced," reasoned Keya.

"I didn't receive any hints that the Bartletts were considering separating," said Inspector Sue, "But we know Malika was working long hours to support her family and she wanted to spend more time with Zaad."

"But she didn't have any choice, did she?" asked Ryan.

"Jonathan isn't getting anywhere with his painting, and he does seem happy not working, and spending time with his son and lunching with the local yummy mummies."

"Malika was stuck," Keya concluded.

"I think you're right," agreed Ryan.

Keya continued, "And if she gave up her job to spend time with her son, they'd have to sell the new house, and lower their outgoings."

"Why not just reduce her working hours?" Ryan asked.

"Perhaps she tried to." concluded Inspector Sue. "Remind me who she works for?"

"Charter, Norris, and Procter. It's an American owned investment company," Ryan replied.

Inspector Sue stood up and stretched her arms into the air.

Then she instructed, "Sergeant Varma. See what you can find out from the company's HR department. Try to persuade them that we don't need a warrant, which technically we do if we want their records. Keep it casual and see if they'll disclose whether or not Malika tried to reduce her working hours or threatened to resign. Meanwhile, Ryan and Stan, I want you to phone around local solicitors to try to find out if Malika approached any of them about divorcing her husband."

"OK," Keya, Ryan and Stan chorused.

"And I'll contact the sister's doctor and see if there's anything I've missed in her records."

Keya was about to look up the details for Charter, Norris, and Proctor when she felt her phone vibrate. Removing it from her pocket, she clicked on the new message and smiled.

Dotty had sent a photo of herself at a castle. Edinburgh Castle, the caption said. Keya did miss her. Dotty would be able to work out what was going on.

Sighing, Keya typed in her password and stared at her computer screen. She searched for Charter, Norris, and Proctor and, when she found their UK website, she scrolled down to the bottom and searched for the human resources, or HR department.

Hesitating, she didn't dial the given number but, instead, undertook another search for members of the department. She didn't want a receptionist deflecting her call, so she needed someone she could ask for by name.

Smiling, she found a page entitled, 'Meet Our People'.

Halfway down it her attention was caught by a photograph of a smiling woman with ebony coloured skin, and a large gold earring. Her face had an open, inviting expression. That's who Keya would speak to.

"Hello," she said when her call was answered, "Please can you put me through to Myriam in HR?"

"One minute," said the receptionist.

"Hello, Myriam Cook."

"Hi, Myriam. My name's Sergeant Keya Varma and I recently helped your colleague, Malika Bartlett, get her son back."

"That was just awful. We felt so bad for her," Myriam replied.

Great. Keya had opened up an informal conversation with the employee. "I know, and it's such a relief to have Zaad back safely. But we need to tie up a few loose ends in the case, so I wondered if you'd mind answering a few questions."

"Well, I'm not sure ..."

"Nothing personal, or anything about her salary or benefits. I'm just trying to find out if Malika requested to work shorter hours, or even if she'd hinted at resigning."

There was a pause before Myriam whispered. "You know we're an American owned company."

"Yes."

"And we have clients globally. Which means account managers are expected to be on call all the time."

"That's hard, especially if you have a family."

"I know," agreed Myriam. "They tried to make me join the night team, but I have a five-year-old daughter."

"What's the night team?" Keya enquired.

"They're the ones who literally work at night, and their members include flexible account managers and admin staff. Don't get me wrong, they are well paid, but my daughter is more important than money."

"I couldn't agree more. I'm of Hindu heritage, so, yes, family is very important."

Miriam lowered her voice even more, and Keya waved her hand at Ryan and Stan, hoping they'd stop talking.

They did, and she was able to catch Myrian say, "I shouldn't tell you this, but Malika has requested on several occasions to work on accounts with either fewer hours, or ones which didn't require evening and weekend working. When her requests were turned down, she asked to work part-time, but that's not really something the company does. I was half-expecting her to submit her resignation papers, as I know she's really struggling with the balance between here and home."

Keya felt there was more, so she waited.

Myriam continued, "And between you and me, her husband not working doesn't help. I think there's tension in that marriage."

"Poor Malika," Keya sympathised. "And then her son being kidnapped this weekend won't have helped."

"Not at all. It's terrible," Myriam agreed. "But at least she's getting the week off. She needs the break. Oh, look, I have to go."

"Thank ..." but the line went dead.

She looked up at Ryan and Stan, who were watching her.

"Sorry for waving my hand at you. I was struggling to hear what the lady from Charter, Norris, and Proctor was saying."

"And what did she say?" asked Stan.

"That Malika has consistently been turned down when she requested to work less or more sociable hours."

"Is that legal these days?" Ryan queried.

"Unfortunately it is," answered Inspector Sue, "if you work for a US based company, you are subject to their employment conditions, which Malika will have signed up to when she joined the company."

Inspector Sue leaned back in her chair. "But working there was impacting on Malika's health. I've just finished speaking to Gamira's doctor. Nothing wrong with her, by the way. But the doctor I spoke to is also Malika's doctor, even though she's now living in Fairford. And she's signed Malika off from work for stress on two occasions in the past nine months, and she's had to prescribe sleeping tablets."

"So Malika is not in a good place," Keya reflected.

"Any luck with solicitors?" Inspector Sue asked.

Ryan and Stan shook their heads.

"Stan, why don't you and I continue with that? Sergeant Varma, take Constable Jenkins and go and pick up the sister. She's in Worcester, but I daren't ask the local police to collect her in case she tips her sister off. If they are involved in this together, we need to be extremely careful. We have to be one hundred per cent certain of Malika's involvement before we arrest her."

Ryan and Keya stood up and Ryan asked, "Can I drive?"

Keya replied, "With pleasure."

CHAPTER FORTY-SIX

Keya and Ryan agreed not to talk about the case on the way to Gamira Jabari's office, located at an office park on the edge of Worcester.

Inspector Sue had rung to confirm Gamira was at work, so Keya relaxed as they drove along the A417, and down the Cotswold escarpment to the M5 motorway.

Turning north, they passed the motorway exit for the M50, which took road users into Wales, and the magnificent Malvern Hills.

Taking the first exit for Worcester, they arrived at the nondescript office park where Gamira worked an hour after leaving the police station.

Entering the glass-fronted foyer, they strode across the marble floor to a curved wooden reception desk. Keya noticed the stares they received because of their police uniforms, but she was used to it. What worried her more was Gamira learning of their arrival.

"You're here to see Gamira, aren't you?" the receptionist asked.

"Yes," Keya replied, uncertainly.

"Mr Rogers asked her to work on a special project in his office. I'll let him know you're coming up. Take the elevator to the third floor. Turn left and his office is on the left."

"Thank you," Keya said, following the receptionist's instructions.

On the third floor, Keya knocked on a pale wooden door with Anthony Rogers engraved on the name plaque.

"Enter," called a male voice.

Keya did so, followed by Ryan, and looked across the office at a serious-looking gentleman in his fifties, sitting behind a black desk.

A young, dark-haired woman, who'd been working at a smaller desk in the corner, glanced up and froze.

"Gamira Jabara, please give me your phone," Keya instructed.

"But …" stammered the young woman, blinking rapidly.

"Your phone," repeated Keya, holding out her hand.

Slowly Gamira picked up her phone and handed it unwillingly to Keya.

"Thank you," said Keya in relief. "Now I'd like you to come to Cirencester Police Station to help us with our enquires."

"No!" Gamira cried.

"I suggest you do as these officers say," said the deep, solemn voice of Mr Rogers.

Gamira shrank back, shaking her head. "I'm not going," she cried.

"Do I have to arrest you and lead you out in handcuffs?" Keya asked, her voice hardening.

Gamira stared at Keya like a frightened animal and slowly shook her head.

"Come on," Ryan said in a friendly voice, as he stepped closer to Gamira. "It's better if you come quietly. We aren't going to hurt you, but I think you know what this is about."

This time Gamira nodded and rose unsteadily to her feet. With Keya in front, and Ryan escorting Gamira, they left the office building and returned to the squad car. They were all silent on the drive back to Cirencester.

Keya entered the team room where Inspector Sue was sitting at her desk, and told her, "Gamira is in interview room 1. Ryan has a better rapport with her than I do, so he's fetching her a cup of tea. She's petrified."

"Did she have a chance to call her sister?"

"No. Her boss had arranged for her to work in his office, and I took her phone away from her the moment we arrived." Keya placed Gamira's phone on Inspector Sue's desk.

"Has she said anything to you?" asked Inspector Sue.

"No, but since she hasn't asked us once what this is about, I think it's clear she knows."

Sue looked down at the notes she'd been writing. "Stan and I haven't had any luck finding a solicitor. Perhaps Malika didn't consult one. But if Ryan and I interview Gamira, can you continue looking? Perhaps you should try Worcester, if that's where she moved from."

"OK," Keya agreed, sitting down behind her desk.

Inspector Sue removed her jacket from its peg and slipped it on before leaving the room.

"Here we are," said Stan, carrying a mug of tea across and placing it on Keya's desk. "Let's see if we can find this solicitor before the inspector and Ryan complete their interview."

Keya hit gold with her third phone call.

"Hello, Whitehaven Solicitors. How can I help you?" said a female voice.

"This is Keya Varma of Cirencester Police. Is Malika Bartlett one of your clients?"

"Yes, she is. Has something happened?" the receptionist replied.

Keya needed to keep her chatting. "Everything's OK now, but her son went missing this weekend."

"The boy on the TV? That was Malika's son?"

"I'm afraid so. We did get him back, but we still have some concerns over his safety, and that of Mrs Bartlett."

"Goodness. I wonder if that's why she consulted Miss Haven."

Keya tapped her keyboard. Annette Haven specialised in divorce and family procedures.

"Can I ask when her last appointment was with Miss Haven?"

Keya heard tapping and then the receptionist replied, "Six weeks ago. I remember now. She was very upset, and understandably so. I made her a cup of tea and she was sobbing about losing her son if she left her husband."

"Why did she think she'd lose him?" asked Keya.

"Because she works, and he's the primary carer. Have you spoken to Mrs Bartlett?"

"Not yet. As you can probably understand, this is a difficult time for her."

"Of course. But she said she was in a real pickle. If she stayed with her husband, she had to work all hours to pay the mortgage on their new house, and fund all his expensive hobbies, and she hardly saw her son.

"But if she divorced her husband, Miss Haven said it was likely he would be granted custody of their son as she'd been working full time, and her husband was, as I've said, the primary carer. So either way, she'd hardly get to see her boy."

"What a predicament," Keya sympathised, hoping the lady would keep talking.

"I know, which is why I suggested she take the boy and run, which I know isn't very professional of me."

"You were only trying to help." Keya knew she should have remonstrated that such an action was illegal.

"I was, wasn't I?"

The lady sounded pleased with herself, and continued, "And then there's the money. Leaving her husband would mean giving him half her assets. She was furious about that. She was having such a rant that I had to show another client into a spare office while he waited to see Mr White.

"But I guess solicitors are like doctors. People only visit them when they have a problem. But I did feel sorry for Mrs Bartlett. I split up with my ex last year, and he's refused to give me a penny. That's why I'm working here, and my son and I are living back with my parents."

Keya thought Malika Bartlett wasn't the only one who needed to verbalise her frustrations and injustices. But the lady had been extremely helpful.

"One last question," said Keya. "Did Mrs Bartlett ever mention her husband physically abusing her or her son?"

"No, but abuse takes many forms, not just physical. For instance, my partner ..."

"Oh, I'm really sorry," interrupted Keya. "My boss is signalling to me," she lied. "Thank you so much for your help, Mrs ?"

"Ms Norton."

"Ms Norton, thank you again."

Keya felt exhausted when she'd finished the call.

Stan looked eagerly at her. "I guess you found the solicitor."

"Yes, that was a lady who works for them, and she had quite a tale to tell."

CHAPTER FORTY-SEVEN

At half past three that afternoon, Ryan drove Inspector Sue, Keya, and Gamira to the Bartletts' house on Cedar Lane.

"I've let her down, haven't I?" sobbed Gamira.

"I only wanted to help. She's been so tired this last year since returning to work after maternity leave. But the company wouldn't let her reduce her hours, and Jonathan wouldn't speak to her for three days after she suggested resigning and finding a job elsewhere."

"Let's talk to your sister," said Inspector Sue, climbing out of the front passenger seat and opening the rear door for Gamira.

Keya, who'd been sitting next to the distressed Gamira, got out and stood beside Ryan.

"Ring the bell, Sergeant," Inspector Sue instructed.

Keya rang the doorbell and stepped back, waiting for someone to answer it.

Biljana did.

Seeing their uniforms, she cried out, "I haven't done anything."

Of course, after her boyfriend's arrest, she probably assumed they were here to arrest her.

"Is Mrs Bartlett in?" Keya asked, keeping her voice level and her tone neutral.

"Malika. Yes, but why do you want to speak to her?"

"That's police business." Keya stepped forward, and Biljana stepped back warily, allowing the police officers and Gamira into the house.

Biljana gasped when she saw Gamira and called out, "Malika, your sister's here."

"What are you doing ..." began Malika as she rushed into the kitchen. She stopped abruptly when she saw Keya and her colleagues.

"I'm so sorry. But they know," sobbed Gamira.

Malika slid to the floor.

Keya and Ryan waited in the kitchen of the Bartletts' house with Gamira. Although unusual, Inspector Sue had thought it best she speak to Malika alone, and she'd called for the duty nurse to come to the house.

"Gami," cried Zaad, rushing into the kitchen from the garden. "Ice cream?"

"Not today, Zaad." The boy looked disappointed, so she asked, "What have you been playing?" He grabbed her hand and started pulling.

Gamira looked round at Keya, who nodded.

"It should be such a happy family scene," Ryan said as they watched Gamira approach a green plastic frog. She clicked a switch and Zaad laughed in delight and started chasing the bubbles the frog machine produced. "Mrs Barlett must have been really desperate to do what she did."

"Pushed to the edge," Keya agreed. "Until she could see no way out."

"Oh, you're back," exclaimed Jonathan Bartlett as he entered the kitchen through the front door.

"Where's my wife?"

"With the inspector," Keya replied.

"Oh. I just wanted to show her my new creation." Jonathan turned a large canvas to face them. It was covered with splashes, smears, and dots of multicoloured paint.

"It looks like something his son painted," whispered Ryan.

There was a knock on the door and a lady dressed in a nurse's uniform entered. Looking at Keya, she said, "Inspector Sue called and asked me to join her to interview a suspect."

"I'll show you through," replied Keya, moving away from the open French windows.

"Suspect? What suspect?" Jonathan asked in confusion.

"Your wife, Mr Bartlett. She's being questioned in relation to the kidnapping of your son, Zaad."

Keya opened the living room door and led the nurse inside.

Malika Bartlett looked as young, frightened, and distressed as Gamira had done earlier.

"I didn't know what else to do," she cried. "Jonathan would have our son and my money, and I would have nothing."

Which wasn't entirely true, thought Keya.

"Which was why you decided to kidnap Zaad?" enquired Inspector Sue.

"It wasn't exactly kidnapping," insisted Malika, as the nurse crossed the room to sit beside her on the sofa. "He was just spending a few days with his favourite aunt."

"But his father didn't know that. And you, or your sister, took him away from the play park without telling Biljana ..."

"That was Gami. She thought it best I wasn't seen," Malika said.

"And you let us all think that he'd been taken by a stranger, and that his life was in danger."

Inspector Sue's tone was not judgemental, but the facts were stark and chilling.

Malika gulped. "When you put it like that."

The nurse took hold of Malika's wrist, presumably to check her pulse, but Malika snatched it away, and like a wild cat, snarled, "Jonathan does nothing for this family but spend my money. He wouldn't hear of me leaving my job.

"He threatened to leave me if I did. And do you know what would happen then? He'd get custody of our son, not me. I was the one who worked so hard to give us this house. This lifestyle. He hasn't earned a penny and just messes about painting those dreadful pictures. But the law said he could take Zaad away from me. Why, then, should I give him half of my hard-earned savings?"

Keya left the living room, closing the door behind her. Ryan was alone in the kitchen.

"Malika has confessed," she told him.

"I would feel sorry for her, as I know how difficult it was for her working long hours and barely seeing her son. But it's the ransom money that gets me, and not wanting her husband to have it. If she had left him, I'm sure she'd have found a new job and she could have applied to the courts again for custody of Zaad, especially if Jonathan wasn't able to provide for him, or he finally had to work and could no longer be the dedicated caregiver."

"But we'll never know," mused Ryan.

"No," Keya agreed. "And we don't know what it's like to believe we're going to lose our only child."

CHAPTER FORTY-EIGHT

"That's the last customer," said an exhausted Monica, the following Saturday evening.

"I can't believe how busy we've been. Do you think anyone noticed that we supplemented the traybakes with cakes from the Women's Institute stall? I'm so sorry I didn't make more."

"Monica, you did an amazing job," Keya praised her.

"What about me?" asked Thomas.

"We couldn't have managed without you." Keya smiled at the teenage boy who seemed to have grown in stature, as well as confidence, since he'd arrived with his mother for his interview at the cafe only a few weeks earlier.

"Did you earn much from the customers' tips?" asked Keya.

"£30," said a delighted Thomas. His face fell. "Does that mean you'll pay me less?"

"Certainly not. In fact, I think you deserve a bonus," said Keya, pushing £50 into his hand.

"Wow, thanks."

"The iced vanilla chai was a popular alternative to tea, especially for those wanting something cooler this afternoon," Monica reported.

"Yes, I think that's something we'll offer in the cafe," Keya agreed.

Gilly and Aunt Beanie approached the white tent from which Keya had been serving afternoon teas.

Aunt Beanie burst out laughing.

"It's not funny," said an indignant Gilly. "Olivia's too young to be drinking, and those boys know better."

"At least it was only boys. Mrs Sawyer told me her niece arranged to meet a boy she'd met online, and he turned out to be a fifty-something man. Luckily, she could run faster than him, but still, it could have led to a nasty incident."

Gilly sighed. "You're right, it could have been much worse. But I do worry when the kids spend so much time on their phones or computers, and they don't always know who they're communicating with."

"Mind you," grinned Aunt Beanie, "I remember when you ..."

"That's quite enough of that," declared Gilly, striding forward. "Thomas, how have you got on?"

"Look at this, Mum?" He waved the banknotes in her face.

"Don't spend it all at once, but off you go and catch up with your friends. I'll meet you back here in, say, half an hour?"

"What about Dad?"

"He had to take Olivia home."

"Why?"

"Never you mind."

Thomas shrugged and rushed off towards the music tent where a band was playing folk music.

"Is there anything left to eat, Keya?" asked Gilly. "I've been on my feet all day."

"Not much, but help yourselves," Keya invited. "There's no point taking it home with us. I'll find some plates."

"And I'll make us all a pot of tea. Vanilla chai OK for everyone?" Monica asked.

"As long as it's hot, wet and sweet, it'll do me," Aunt Beanie confirmed.

At the back of the tent, Keya said to Monica, "I might as well put what's left onto plates and everyone can help themselves." She placed all the remaining food onto four plates and carried them out to Gilly and Aunt Beanie, who were sitting down, soaking up the early evening sun.

"What have you got there?" asked Monica, as Ryan appeared carrying a plastic bag, which seemed to be holding some sort of electronic equipment.

"There's a man here selling all sorts of computer equipment from the 80s and 90s. It's so retro.

Aunt Beanie raised her eyebrows.

"Grab yourself a plate and help yourself to some more food,' Monica said to Ryan.

"And then you and Keya can tell us exactly who you've arrested this week and why. Ronnie Marsh wrote a piece in the Cirencester Times about the kidnapped boy case, but I'm sure most of it isn't true," said Gilly.

Monica leaned forward and said, "But he did write a lovely piece for Cotswold Life about Keya's cafe."

"Yes, but back to the Bartletts," insisted Aunt Beanie. "Are you certain the mother was behind it all?"

Keya picked up a cheddar cheese, celery, and onion chutney sandwich and said, "I'm afraid so."

She bit into the sandwich and thought while she chewed.

Then she continued, "When Malika returned to work after maternity leave, she really struggled. They'd bought the house in Fairford so she would be closer to the office, and to cut down on her commuting time, but she was still expected to work long, and often anti-social hours. She and Jonathan had waited to have children until they were financially stable, but Malika missed Zaad terribly when she went back to work."

"I bet it didn't help that her useless husband was gadding about visiting art exhibitions and lunching all over the county," Aunt Beanie pointed out.

"No, it didn't, and Malika's resentment grew until, she admitted to us, she finally realised he had no intention of being a serious artist. He just dabbled for show so she wouldn't get annoyed with him."

"Shame. He could draw," Aunt Beanie conceded.

Keya nodded. "That's what Jarrod said. But Jonathan didn't put any effort into it. What he did do was spend more and more of

Malika's hard-earned money. When they were at the cafe a few weeks ago, he was trying to persuade her to buy a Porsche Cayenne. Not a new one, but still, a very expensive car."

"But why didn't Mrs Bartlett just leave her husband?" asked Monica.

"Because her solicitor advised her that Jonathan would get custody of Zaad, as he'd been looking after the boy while she worked, as well as half their, or rather her, assets."

"Why didn't she give up her job, and use her share of their savings to get settled and reapply to have Zaad?" Gilly asked.

"I think, in a way, that's what she did decide to do," Keya considered.

"She knew Jonathan would get half the house, although that isn't as much as you'd think after the mortgage has been paid off, but she drew the line at her hard-earned savings and investments. Which is when she devised the kidnapping plan. She admitted it was supposed to be low key, and not involve the police, and she'd pay herself the £250,000 as a ransom, and then quit her job."

"That's quite clever really," agreed Aunt Beanie. "But she was wrong to involve her son."

"She didn't see any other way," Keya confided.

"And now she'll lose everything. Her son, her freedom, and the money," Monica said.

"Not the money," replied Ryan. "That's disappeared. Which was her sister, Gamira's doing."

"But what's the use of money when you're stuck in prison?" insisted Aunt Beanie.

"Poor woman. She probably just needed someone to talk to," Gilly sympathised.

"I saw Jason with his mother and Biljana throwing balls to knock coconuts off their poles at the coconut shy," said Ryan.

"He's a lucky man," Aunt Beanie asserted. "A two-year suspended sentence and a hundred and twenty hours of community service. I hope he's learned his lesson."

"He's doing some of his community hours at the church, and some more picking up litter and helping at Akemans," said Gilly.

"How is being at Akemans community work?" asked Aunt Beanie.

"I think we're a community, aren't we? And we help each other." Gilly smiled at the group.

"I visited Inspector Evans' mum in hospital," Aunt Beanie said, changing the subject. "Her hip operation went OK, but she's completely bonkers now. She kept telling me a rabbit was nibbling her toes, and a monkey was sitting on my shoulder."

"Peter said that's the general anaesthetic. It can seriously affect older people, and their hallucinations can last several months," Gilly explained.

"I hope someone tells the inspector that. He's going mad pretending to move birds off his head and shoo deer away from his mother's hospital bed."

Keya smiled at the image.

"And we solved a case without Chief Inspector Greg, who is still enjoying his holiday in the Lake District with his family," Ryan reflected.

"That's good," Monica agreed.

"I'd like to visit the Lake District," said Keya in a dreamy voice.

"Always rains," declared Aunt Beanie.

"We had a lovely holiday there when you were younger, Ryan." Monica clasped her son's hand. "Sometimes I think it's a shame children have to grow up."

"But you've done a great job, Monica," acknowledged Aunt Beanie. "Ryan is a level-headed young man. And he's doing an excellent job in the police force."

Monica beamed, "Thank you."

Aunt Beanie added. "Now all he needs to do is find a worthy young woman to marry."

Gilly and Aunt Beanie turned to look at Keya.

Blushing, she replied, "Don't look at me. I'm far too old for him."

Gilly sighed, "That's a shame. You work well together. Now we have to find you both suitable partners."

"I think we should be grateful for what we have. Especially our friends," declared Aunt Beanie.

Keya raised her delicate floral teacup and replied, "I'll drink to that."

Chamomile Tea and A Copycat Crime

Can Keya continue juggling her police work with running her cafe? And as her younger sister is happily married, does she need some love in her life? Find out in her next book.

A body in the Cotswolds. A cryptic floral clue. Can a budding community cop unearth the secrets of a 40-year-old case before the truth withers away?

Claim your copy of Chamomile Tea and A Copycat Crime

Hour is Come

Would you like to read Keya's first case with her friend Dotty? And discover how The Waterwheel Cafe and Dotty Sayers Antique Mystery series began?

Find out and download *Hour is Come,* which is yours to keep when you sign up to my newsletter for updates.

Claim your copy of Hour is Come

Fake Death

Have you read the first book in the Dotty Sayers Antique Mystery series?

Young widow, Dotty Sayers, is delighted with her new auction house job in Britain's picturesque Cotswolds. But she's shocked by a soldier's death on Remembrance Day. She realises appearances can be deceiving, but can she track down the real culprit and prevent an innocent man from imprisonment?

Claim Your Copy of Fake Death

If you enjoyed this book, please tell someone you know. And for those people you don't know, leave a review to help them decide whether or not to read it.

Review on Amazon

For more information visit VictoriaTait.com

UNTITLED

Printed in Great Britain
by Amazon

55876568R00126